FERRON'S JOURNEY

PART TWO: HIDDEN

JP SAYLE

FERRON'S JOURNEY: PART 2 HIDDEN

Will close proximity to Isaac get Ferron to finally see what is right in front of him?

The moment Isaac lays eyes on Ferron, he is entranced, but instead of showing his interest he stays in the background. But then fate steps in and Isaac fears he's lost his chance forever.

That is, until he is given a golden opportunity.

With Ferron living in his home, Isaac gets more than he bargained for when Ferron's past mistakes come back to haunt them both. After Ferron's confession, will Isaac stand and fight or go back to hiding in the background?

Ferron's Journey: Hidden Part Two, The Playroom series (Book 5) is an MM gay suspense romance with a Daddy desperate to show his love to a lost boy. Is close proximity the answer to a damaged soul?

This is the second part of a trilogy and the author advises that they should be read in order to properly under-

stand the story. This book has aspects of a non-consensual relationship with possible triggers due to scenes of abuse.

Books Character Family Tree

Below are the characters that can be found in other books and series written or being written in 2020.

Isaac (Bar Manager of The Playroom, Ferron's partner)—Dominated but not Subdued: La Trattoria Di Amore Series (book 2), Mine, Body and Soul Trilogy: The Playroom Series. Ferron's Journey Part One: Damaged, The Playroom Series (Book 4).

Ferron (Bartender in The Playroom, Isaac's partner)—La Trattoria Di Amore series book 1&2, Mine, Body and Soul Trilogy: The Playroom Series. Ferron's Journey Part One: Damaged, The Playroom Series.

Scott (Waiter in LTDA, partner Luke)—La Trattoria Di Amore Series (book 1&2), Mine, Body and Soul Trilogy, The App: Daddy Kink (book 1), Always More (book 1) The Flamingo Bar Series. The App: Littles (book 2), The Little Side of Me, (book 2) The Flamingo Bar release date October.

Adam (Floor Manager of LTDA, partner Carl)—La Trattoria Di Amore Series (book 1), Main Character Dominated but not Subdued: La Trattoria Di Amore, (book 2), Mine, Body and Soul Trilogy, The App: Daddy Kink (book 1)

Carl — (Head Chef of LTDA and Co-owner of The Playroom, partner Adam)—La Trattoria Di Amore Series (book 1), Main Character Dominated but not Subdued: La Trattoria Di Amore, (book 2), Mine, Body and Soul Trilogy, The App: Daddy Kink (book 1)

Nathan — (Co-owner of The Playroom, partner Lenny)—La Trattoria Di Amore Series (book 1 & 2), Main Character Mine, Body and Soul Trilogy, The App: Daddy Kink (book 1), The App: Littles (book 2), The Little Side of Me, (book 2) The Flamingo Bar release date October.

Lenny — (Trainee Chef of LTDA, partner Nathan) La Trattoria Di Amore Series (book 1 & 2), Main Character Mine, Body and Soul Trilogy, The App: Daddy Kink (book 1), The Little Side of Me, (book 2) The Flamingo Bar release date October.

Bailey — Part Three Mine Body and Soul: The Playroom Series, Ferron's Journey Part Two: Hidden, The Playroom series. He will get a book (no date as yet but it will be the third book in The App Series).

Richie (Office assistant LTDA, partner Seb)—Main Character La Trattoria Di Amore Series (book 1), La Trattoria Di Amore, (book 2), Mine, Body and Soul Trilogy, The App: Daddy Kink (book 1)

Sebastian (Co-owner of LTDA restaurants with

Carl, partner Richie)—Main Character La Trattoria Di Amore Series (book 1), La Trattoria Di Amore, (book 2), Mine, Body and Soul Trilogy, The App: Daddy Kink (book 1), The Manx Cat Guardians (book 7)

Theo — **(Waiter in LTDA)**—La Trattoria Di Amore Series (book 1&2), Mine, Body and Soul Trilogy: The Playroom Series. Ferron's Journey Part One: Damaged, The Playroom Series (book 4)

Sawyer — **(Waiter in LTDA, partner Boyd)**—Main Character The App: Littles (book 2) The Little Side of Me, (book 2) The Flamingo Bar release date October. The App: Daddy Kink, (book 1), La Trattoria Di Amore Series book 1 &2, Mine, Body and Soul part one, two and three, The Playroom Series.

Boyd — **(Construction Owner, partner Sawyer)**—Mine, Body and Soul Trilogy: The Playroom Series, Main Character The App: Littles (book 2). The Little Side of Me, (book 2) The Flamingo Bar release date October.

Sometimes life takes us on an unexpected journey that we think is wrong, but maybe it was to teach us a lesson.

Prologue

New Year

Isaac

The smell of disinfectant, along with other things I didn't even want to think about, wafted on the warm air as the door opened and one of the nurses I'd seen earlier walked through into the visitors' waiting area. I'd been sat on a seat that wasn't built for a man my size for four hours just for the chance to have five minutes with Ferron.

Used to the feeling of disappointment as they took other visitors and left me sitting there, I went back to staring at the drab cream wall in front of me. For days I'd been coming to sit and wait in this shoebox of a room, tantalisingly close to the intensive care unit just for the opportunity to see Ferron, to touch him, to let him know I was there for him.

You failed him, why would he care if you're here?

I pushed my palms against my thighs as the urge to punch something, *anything*, rose swiftly. My promises to keep him safe had been about as useful as an umbrella in a force ten gale. They'd done nothing to protect him. *Fuck no!* I'd allowed that bastard, Devon, to waltz right in under my nose and take... take what?

Take what? You've spent years watching him, yearning for him, and look what happened!

Ferron was lying unconscious in an intensive care bed, the same place he'd been ever since New Year's Eve after his ex, Devon had...

"Mr. Corrigan, would you come with me please? We really need your help."

It took a second to register that the nurse hadn't gone over to the two women clutching each other's hands. Instead she was standing in front of me, her pinched expression causing me to lurch out of my seat. "What is it? Ferron... Is Ferron okay?" Emotion thickened my throat and I willed myself to keep it together.

"He's starting to wake up and sometimes people get distressed in unfamiliar surroundings. But he's... well, he's more distressed than we'd expect." She spoke in a lowered tone, encouraging me to follow her into the unit. As the waiting room door closed behind us, she continued, "We're hoping your presence will help to calm him down."

At the sound of mewling coming from Ferron's bed, any thought of explaining why he might be distressed after what I'd seen on the recording, fled. I didn't hesitate, passing the nurse before she could say anything else. My sole focus was on the man in the bed.

His battered face was twisted into an expression I'd hoped to never see again. His terror was suffocating as machines beeped alarmingly. Several people were stood around, none of them appearing to do anything to help.

Without saying a word, I went over to the bed and crouched down, gently cupping his grossly swollen and bruised cheek. "I'm here, little man. I'm here... take a breath for me," I coaxed, speaking softly into his ear.

Once he'd stopped fighting and was sagging against the bed, one of the nurses pressed a button on the machine attached to the needle in his arm. His eyelashes fluttered, his lips parting as his jaw went lax.

"What have you given him?" I demanded in a tight voice barely recognisable as my own. I stood, towering over Ferron's bed.

"It's analgesia to help with the pain," she answered immediately, moving closer to the bed to readjust one of the tubes. "The doctor was a little reluctant to give him a dose when he was showing signs of waking up. But then he got a little panicked, which can happen. Although, it seems all he needed was your touch." She gave me a gentle smile.

I stiffened as I examined her face. When all I could see was genuine concern though, without any condemnation, I nodded. An odd beeping noise had her looking back at one of the monitors before I could say more. Her attention back on her job, I considered the last time anyone had shown any interest in my sexual orientation.

I'd long ago got used to people's differing reactions about me being gay. I'd been in my teens when I'd figured out what I was into, and it wasn't girls or vanilla sex. The considerable media focus on HIV at the time had frightened my parents when I'd told them about my sexual orientation. They'd been shocked, but they were more concerned whether I might contract a disease that could kill me. After educating themselves though, they'd eventually become more relaxed about it, all except for my grandparents on my mother's side. It had been hard going as a teenager when they'd visited and treated me like some sort of bug carrier. They'd even refused to touch anything I might have had my hands on. My mother had eventually stopped inviting them to special occasions so that they couldn't spoil it for everyone.

I supposed though, that the experience had prepared me for being recruited into the Special Forces where men were equally as ignorant. I'd initially signed up to the Navy wanting to be a submariner, but as it had become apparent that I had strategic combat skills, I'd found my career going down a different path. A path that had led to men attempting to show me what happened to a gay man in their unit.

They'd quickly discovered what I could do though, and what happened if they messed with me. I gave a humourless chuckle at the memory. The nurse shifting caught my attention and as I met her gaze, her brow arched. I scratched my head. Had I missed something? "Yes, it appears my presence does help him. At least now I'm allowed in!" I replied, the bite of anger still present in my voice after all the hoops they'd made me jump through in order to see Ferron.

A faint blush appeared on her face, but she didn't respond to my dig. "Why don't you grab the seat over there and hold his hand? Touch can be very therapeutic to patients." I took the olive branch she'd offered and went over to grab the chair against the wall.

Each space was laid out the same, with the bed in the middle of the floor space. Machines were situated on either side of the bed, some attached to poles while others were on the floor. Behind the bed were large windows that let in light, but the view was only of brick walls and sky.

As I sat, the residual anger tasted bitter on my tongue. The hospital had been dead set against me getting anywhere near Ferron to start with, their protocols stating that it was next of kin only. So I'd had to prove that Ferron lived with me, and that I, for all intents and purposes, was his next of kin.

I'd been grateful that Nathan, my boss, had missed my epic meltdown. He'd been occupied elsewhere with Lenny, his injured boyfriend. The fact that I'd managed to keep it together throughout the whole ordeal was still a miracle. But with Nathan still distraught over Lenny being kidnapped along with Ferron, one of us had needed to keep their head. Not that that had been easy after watching the fucker take what we held most precious in the world and subject it to a vicious attack. It had taken every bit of my training to keep myself under control as the bastard had ripped my world open, tearing away hopes and dreams that I'd harboured for many years. Dreams I'd held close to my chest from the very first moment I'd ever laid eyes on Ferron.

Memories of that day flooded my mind.

I wiped at the spilt beer on the bar, looking up and offering a smile to the next customer. "What can I get...?"

Eyes as bright as blue sky stared at me nervously, stealing my ability to find oxygen in the room. The hand holding the cloth clenched until my knuckles turned white as I dropped my gaze back to the bar, my train of thought lost. Heat rode up my neck and I swallowed hard before forcing myself to look back at the most alluring face I'd ever seen. Urges I tended to ignore surfaced fast. My initial search for the perfect boy when I'd first joined the scene had drawn a big, fat blank so I'd buried the need. At least until now. Now, all I could picture was the man who stood in front of me curled up in my lap and looking up at me with those adorable eyes.

Fuck!

I hadn't even realised he wasn't alone until the friend stood next to him nudged him. My eyes narrowed on the other guy as I recalled who he was: Wren. He was a sub that I'd contracted for a night or two. Wren was a pain slut and he'd been more than willing to take what I'd dished out. My gaze moved back to the man fidgeting at Wren's side. Was this guy into the same thing? Was he only after someone to dish out pain? The thought depressed me and I had to work hard not

to let my shoulders drop. *"What can I get you guys to drink?"
I glanced between both men, my brows rising in question.*

*"Do you have a cocktail menu?" was the timid response
from the unknown guy.*

*"Hold up. I'll grab you one." I swung around to get one.
His voice was like warm, melted honey, my groin flooding
with heat. I inhaled a shaky breath as my gaze met the guy's
in the mirror behind the bar, holding mine for the longest
second before his chin dipped and he broke the connection.*

The seat squeaked as I shifted on it, blinking Ferron's
sleeping form back into focus. The feelings he'd wrought
in me from that first night had never faded. In fact, over
time they'd grown stronger and taken root, bringing with
it a fear of the unknown, a part of me instantly recog-
nising that he'd change my world. Only I'd been too
chicken shit to do anything about it.

While I'd hesitated, Ferron had set his sights on Carl.
So I'd kept my growing feelings to myself, watching as
Carl crushed Ferron's hopes for anything more than play
dates. Then Ferron had disappeared, not contacting
anyone for months. Nathan had mentioned in passing
that he'd seen him with a Dom. A Dom who'd turned
out to be a crazy motherfucker and the reason why
Ferron was in the hospital. I pushed the hair back off his
face gently, tracing a finger down over the lurid bruising.
Anger sizzled in my gut, but I kept my touch gentle.

Were we ever going to catch a break? Would Ferron
ever see what had been right in front of him for the
whole time: me.

Chapter One

Isaac

"Will you stop please, Isaac! I know you're worried about me, but I have to go to my appointment and I can't delay any longer or I'll be late." Ferron's left eye ticked, the muscle jumping erratically. It was something I'd come to notice that happened when he got pissed at me. That tick had had quite the workout over the last couple of weeks, what with my Daddy nature none too happy with some of Ferron's actions. His cajoling tone did nothing to alleviate the tension holding my neck and shoulders hostage.

The minute he'd mentioned going to the appointment—alone, I'd got a bad feeling about it. I wasn't sure whether it was just the protective urges that had increased tenfold since his release from hospital, or if it was something more. With him acting jumpier than a cat on a hot tin roof, I couldn't figure it out. My whole mission in life had become to wrap him in cotton wool and keep him safe. I'd failed him once and I had no intention of letting it happen again.

"Can't you give it a few more minutes until Nathan arrives, then I can go with you?"

His eye roll and huff made my palm itch with the urge to spank his bum for being a naughty boy. *He's not your boy, remember!*

I refused to back down though. "A few more minutes, that's all I'm asking for."

He shook his head, stamping his foot on the ground. "We're just going round the houses. I'm going, so get over it."

He poked his chin out at me, the wealth of love and pride I felt at that action stopping me from arguing any further. That little show of defiance demonstrated how far he'd come from the cowering man he'd been after leaving Devon. I'd been worried after what had happened at New Year that we'd be back to where he'd been before the attack. But although he'd had his moments, they'd lessened over time.

I still couldn't help showing my disappointment though as he put his jacket on. "Alright, go. But... be careful," I tagged on lamely as he spun around and stomped over to the door without looking back.

Once he'd gone, my disheartened sigh echoed around the empty bar. To keep myself busy, I stocked the shelves with the bottles Ferron had brought earlier from the stockroom. Nathan arrived a few minutes later, sitting at the bar to go through the daily list of topics we usually discussed. I found myself struggling to pay attention though. The sense of foreboding wouldn't leave. Every time Ferron was out of my sight, I couldn't settle. It was worse now that I knew he was roaming around London on his own.

"What is it with you? Twice I've asked you a question and twice you haven't even bothered to look at me," Nathan said, sounding more than a little miffed at being ignored.

"What was your question?"

"Have you put the advert out yet for the new bar staff we'll need for the Flamingo Bar?" he said, following it with a huff.

"Yep, did it last week. We've had about fifteen applications to date, some of which actually look promising." I rubbed my jaw and then the nape of my neck, a tingling feeling spreading down my spine. What was wrong with me?

Ferron is alone in London.

My gut clenched.

No matter how much I'd promised to keep him safe, I'd failed him. Nothing would change that, no matter what Nathan said. He was the only one who knew about my past and the skills I had. Had they done me any good when the fucker had got into the building right under our noses and kidnapped Ferron and Lenny? That question continued to haunt me when the obvious answer was—no.

"If you don't stop brooding, I'm gonna suggest we go up to the boxing ring so I can knock some fucking sense into you. Is this about Ferron going to his appointment on his own?"

I glared at Nathan. "Maybe. He left ten minutes ago in a huff because I showed concern about him not having anyone with him." My teeth ground together at the memory of how much I'd wanted to demand that I go with him.

"What has you spooked? Devon is behind bars. He can't touch Ferron." Nathan's brows rose questioningly.

"I... I just feel that there's more to this whole thing with Devon. Ferron isn't telling us something. He's hiding something. But what?" I shook my head, my unease growing with every passing second. "I feel like something is about to go down, and for the life of me, I'm struggling to figure out why I feel like that." I shrugged. "Am I just overreacting or..." I trailed off as Nathan's face became thoughtful.

"Your spidery senses have saved your butt more than once. Go with it. If you wanna follow Ferron, go. I'll sort stuff here and"—Nathan waved at the invoices scattered across the bar— "finish this lot."

I all but ran to grab my jacket. I was out of the door quickly, rushing down the street towards the tube station and praying that Ferron hadn't gone so far that I couldn't catch up with him.

The streets teemed with people as I dodged and ran around them in my rush to follow Ferron to his appointment. Even in the icy cold, sweat coated my skin as I sped up and took the route that would take me to the psychologist's office at London Bridge.

I squinted at the crossing up ahead. Was that Ferron? My blood throbbed inside my skull, making my ears ring as I caught another glimpse of what appeared to be Ferron's jacket. Then the crowd swelled and surged forward into the road, Ferron looking as if he was going to fall until a man grabbed hold of his arm.

For a moment I lost sight of him as I skidded around someone. But then he reappeared. The brief flare of joy at catching up with him soon disappeared though. My eyes widened, my brain struggling to compute why the man was continuing to hold Ferron. Jealousy swam thickly through my veins and I found it impossible to take a breath. Was this why he hadn't wanted me to accompany him? Had he planned on meeting another man for a... date? The other guy was clearly a Dom, his whole demeanour screamed it.

My mouth thinned, but before I could chastise myself for being such a fool to think that I could claim Ferron as my own, there was a loud shout of, "no... no!"

Ferron! Oh fuck, Ferron!

Icy terror tried to take charge, but I shoved it firmly aside as I barrelled into people in my haste to get to Ferron. The man who held his arm was dragging him towards a sleek black car sat at the curb.

"Stop them!" I shouted, fear of him getting Ferron into the car before I could get to him driving my actions. Several people started to pay attention as Ferron fought with the guy. I bellowed as I watched a fist fly towards

Ferron's face. Blood smeared his mouth, his head lolling back and his legs crumpling.

I leapt into the road with a total disregard for the moving traffic, Ferron my only focus. Several horns blared as cars screeched to a stop, but I barely noticed. The man holding a now limp Ferron in his arms glanced my way at the commotion, his eyes wild as he released him. A cry fell from my lips, my heart stuttering in my chest as Ferron fell to the ground in a heap. The legs of a nearby stranger were the only thing that stopped his head from hitting the tarmac.

I was dimly aware of the noise of a revving engine as I fell to my knees and took hold of Ferron. "Ferron, Ferron can you hear me?" I rasped out past my dry throat.

I stared at his face, exhaling in a rush as his eyelashes fluttered open to reveal dazed eyes. My sinuses burned and my eyes ached. Overwhelmed with emotion, I lowered my forehead to his, needing a second to get myself under control before I confessed how I really felt to him. "You know, if you keep this up I'm going to turn grey," I muttered as I lifted my head.

His eyes met mine and my heart trembled at his words.

"I'm sorry, Daddy."

Chapter Two

Ferron

I'd vaguely heard Isaac ask for someone to ring for an ambulance and the police. Although I'd wanted to argue that I was okay and we didn't need the police, it had only taken one look at the rigid set of Isaac's jaw to dissuade me. He was in full Daddy Dom mode and there was no way I was going to be able to make him listen.

How was I going to explain this? I had so many secrets and where had they got me? Lying on a street with yet more blood spilt. Would this torment ever end? A sob became stuck in my throat at the thought of what I'd kept hidden.

Hidden. The word threatened to break through the thin barrier I'd erected to stop me thinking about what the guy would have done if he'd succeeded in getting me into his car. Was he after revenge for what had happened to Devon? Or was it something more? Why had I ever gone to that stupid club? *Why?*

A shiver ran through my body, the cold from the ground penetrating through my jeans and numbing my arse. The throbbing ache behind my eyes increased to add to my woes. I closed them, hoping I could block everything out, hoping I could block the whole world out. I tightened my grip on Isaac's coat, the scent of his aftershave helping me to remember that I was surrounded by my happy place, regardless of the fact that I was half-lying on the pavement with people staring at me.

As the minutes slipped by, I let the sounds of traffic and voices distract me as Isaac's strong arms held onto me. I snuggled into him, his arms tightening and his chin dropping onto the top of my head. My heart fluttered madly, feeling as if it had filled my chest to capacity. It reminded me of a scene at a butterfly sanctuary that I'd visited on holiday in Rhodes. Someone had made a loud noise and thousands of butterflies had taken to the sky in fright. Their tiny wings had beat wildly to give a spectacular show as they'd filled the air until they were all you could see and hear.

"Are you warm enough?" Isaac murmured. His voice rumbled inside his chest that was right next to my head.

I nodded, lifting my eyelids with effort as I gazed up at him. The feeling in my chest only increased in response to the concern etched in his eyes and the questions I could see there. I licked my dry lips, a metallic taste flooding my mouth. My stomach heaved, making me try and sit up. The pain in my jaw kept me from focusing properly as I tried to swallow the gathering saliva in my mouth.

I used the waves of nausea to push away the unspoken question between Isaac and myself. Had I called him Daddy because my brain had been addled by the punch, or was it because that's how I saw him?

You know you've wanted him to be your Daddy ever since he first mentioned it, so stop pretending.

The sound of sirens stopped me from examining too closely what my head was trying to tell me.

As I was loaded into the back of an ambulance, I heard Isaac telling the paramedic in no uncertain terms that he was coming with me. My lips twitched, but I was too exhausted to smile as Isaac stepped into the back of the ambulance with a disgruntled looking paramedic. As the warmth inside the vehicle began to heat my body, it also signalled where all the new bruises were going to be. The journey to the hospital felt never-ending as I was poked and prodded. Then the paramedic brought out the dreaded needle to stick in me.

I sucked in a shaky breath, blanching as the guy wiggled the needle into my vein. I scrunched my eyes shut as tears slid down my cheeks.

"Hold my hand, little man. Come on, focus on me."

The use of his Daddy voice was enough to make me obey. "I don't like needles Da..." My eyes widened and I pinched my lips together at my near slip up. Heat flooded my cheeks as I stared up at Isaac, begging him to forgive me.

What was wrong with me? Was I defective in some way?

"All done," the paramedic announced in a far too jovial voice as if he'd sensed the rising tension. He stood, or as much as he could in the ambulance, gathering the bits of rubbish together from the trolley I lay on. Then he proceeded to ask me several questions about what I could remember and where the pain was. I remembered none of the last ambulance ride, so I tried to answer his questions without giving too much away.

"Stop evading, little man. That won't help them to treat you," Isaac grumbled as he squeezed my fingers just hard enough to get me to focus.

"Sorry... I... the pain." I stopped as Isaac's brow rose, the creases around his eyes deepening.

He switched his attention immediately to the paramedic. "Can you give him something?"

"Yes, I can." He looked at me with a warm smile on his face. "Are you allergic to anything?"

"Not that I'm aware of."

The guy nodded and reached for a green box, opening it to draw some clear liquid into a syringe. The whole time Isaac watched him like a hawk would watch its prey.

After the paramedic had administered the drug, things got real floaty and I wasn't sure if I'd drifted to sleep or not because the next thing I knew I was in the emergency department. Isaac was standing at the end of the trolley I lay on, talking to a man dressed in dark green scrubs.

I started to cough as I tried to swallow past my dry throat, both men's gaze shifting to me.

"Hello, Ferron. I'm Dr White. How are you feeling?" He smiled warmly at me as he moved to within arms' reach.

"I'm a little groggy, but I think that's whatever they gave me in the ambulance for the pain. Can I go home?" I tagged the question on at the end because, for me, that was the most important part. The last thing I wanted was to be stuck in the hospital again because of Devon, even though it was his friends this time rather than him. It was all the same to me; they were all part of the same nightmare.

He gave a wry chuckle. "Well, let me examine you first. Then we can talk about it." He took hold of my wrist, his fingers resting there for a moment as I assumed he was taking my pulse.

I silently cursed as the blasted thing beat erratically, blood bouncing around my veins like a child on a trampoline. He released my wrist but didn't say anything, lifting the stethoscope from around his neck to continue his examination.

By the time he'd finished, I was sweating and my hands were trembling from the questions about my head, my memory and the events which had led up to me being in hospital.

"Do you have someone you can stay with for the next twenty-four to forty-eight hours? Although, I can't find anything wrong and the head x-ray doesn't show any fractures, I'm concerned that you lost consciousness for a few minutes. I'd prefer that you have someone stay with you to keep an eye out for signs of concussion."

My eyes narrowed as he spoke. Had I had a head x-ray? Crikey, the stuff they'd given me in the ambulance must have been good shit if I couldn't even remember having my head x-rayed.

"—that will be fine then," Dr White said, glancing between me and Isaac.

What was fine? What had I missed? I shook my head, regretting it as fresh pain throbbed to life. My teeth ground together to stop a whimper as my neck muscles spasmed to express how unhappy they were with me. I lifted my hand to rub my nape trying to act normal.

The doctor disappeared beyond the trolley curtain. "What is fine? Can I go home?" The thickness in my voice couldn't be helped, but I still worked to keep my face neutral as Isaac moved over to where the doctor had previously stood.

His fathomless dark eyes raked over my face before holding my gaze. "You *can* go home because I'll be there to take care—"

"What! You have work. What will Nathan say?" I cried out in panic. I was too freaked-out to take much notice of the way Isaac's lips pursed and his eyes grew darker.

Shit, shit, shit!

Now I was going to get Isaac into trouble. It was bad enough that I wasn't fit enough to go into work myself and finish my shift. I'd contemplated it for a whole three seconds, but with my head feeling as if it had been through an old-fashioned clothes mangle, there was no way I could manage to keep it together for the remainder of my shift. But I didn't want to think about Nathan having to contend with both of us not returning. I cringed. Would Nathan decide I wasn't worth the trouble?

You aren't worth anything. Devon's insidious voice crept past my defences.

Any hope of keeping my emotions in check withered at the mental attack. My nerves took control of my mouth and through the tears clogging my throat, I began to ramble, "I'm sorry, I am. Please go to work. I'll be fine, I swear." The fact that my stomach knotted at the idea at being left on my own was irrelevant. I just needed to ensure that Isaac's Daddy side didn't cloud his judgement.

"Little man, shush now." Isaac's voice was firm but without any censure as he took hold of my trembling hands. His thumbs lazily grazed over my knuckles in gentle circles. "I've sorted it with Nathan. He's fine with me taking the next couple of days as holiday. I've spoken to the police and they'll come by the house tomorrow. I need to be there for that too. So you see, there's nothing for you to get upset about. I'll enjoy a few lazy days while I get you to run around after me baking treats. It's win-win for me." He gave a cheeky grin.

Some of the tension gripping my shoulders released at the humour dancing in his eyes. "Okay... okay, I can do that..." I swallowed the next word on the tip of my tongue.

Isaac's face fell for a second, but before I'd even had a chance to blink he'd turned his head away as if he was searching for something in the cubicle.

Was he disappointed that I'd not called him Daddy like I'd wanted to? As he continued to look anywhere but at me, I pushed the idea away though, telling myself that I was reading far too much into his distraction.

Chapter Three

Isaac

The sound of clattering pots in the kitchen distracted me from the book I'd been reading, my lips curling into a smile. Well, I'd been attempting to read. Normally the latest thriller by Tess Gerritsen would have had me gripped from the first page, but with the sounds and scents coming from my kitchen for the last hour, I'd found it difficult to concentrate.

What about Ferron calling you, Daddy? Isn't that what's distracting you?

Seriously, let it be.

He'd been laid out cold by a punch and clearly not in his right mind when he came to.

What about the second time in the back of the ambulance? What about then?

How fucking old are you? Quit with the guessing games, and just come right out and ask him.

I blew out a breath as I thought about the way I'd been going round and round in circles in an attempt to do exactly that. Every time I looked at the lurid purple bruising covering his lower cheek and jaw, my heart squeezed with terror. Besides, if he said he was mine, it would only lift the lid on my anger. Anger that had been bubbling ever since he'd refused to talk to the police and give them information on the man who'd assaulted him. I'd been so focused on Ferron at the time that I'd barely registered much about the guy and the black car he'd driven off in.

I stared at the open book in front of me without seeing the words. Was there something I was missing?

I suspected that the answer was, yes. That I'd been missing something important the whole time. But what was it? Why wouldn't Ferron talk about it? What would stop someone from talking? Fear? Threats?

My brow furrowed, sweat beading on my top lip. Was that it? Had he been threatened? I cursed, recalling the lack of sound from the video feed on the night he and Lenny had been taken.

Maybe I needed to examine it again? To see if I'd missed anything important. My stomach churned at the idea, but with Ferron remaining tight-lipped, I didn't think I had any other option.

Yeah, whatever had happened, Ferron was keeping it to himself. Well, not totally to himself. He was talking to his psychologist. I tried to push aside the jealousy sliding greasily around the pit of my stomach, knowing it was irrational. The guy wanted to help Ferron and at least he was speaking to someone, right? But why wasn't he speaking to me? Why didn't he trust me?

You failed him, remember. You promised to keep him safe and you didn't. So why would he trust you?

The truth was a hard pill to swallow. I rose up off the sofa, dropping the book onto the large coffee table. The *thud* barely registered past my growing disquiet. How could I fix it?

Show him how you feel.

Fuck, no!

The 'fuck no' was immediate. My hands clenched into fists as I stalked over to the large window and looked out over the Downs. The dark grey sky matched my gloomy mood as I stared out.

It was easy to understand why I'd shied away from making a commitment, what with the years of never knowing if I'd get to come home after being sent out on a perilous mission. It had made it impossible to keep a long-term relationship going. I'd tried, but maybe not hard enough. Since I'd started working for Nathan, I'd stuck to BDSM contracts and found that they suited just fine.

Or at least they had until Ferron had joined the club and he'd called to me. But I'd still not taken the initiative. With him living under my roof, I'd had plenty of time to examine why that was. It was fear—pure and simple. It lurked in the recesses of my mind. Fear that I couldn't be what he wanted, that I wouldn't be enough for him. It controlled me more than I wanted to admit. In the middle of the night with his scent still lingering, there was no escape from my fears.

Such close proximity to what I wanted was like water torture, especially when as each day passed he endeared himself to me more and more. His sweet nature, his need to please, his desire to be taken care of made him the perfect boy. Breath hissed through my clenched teeth fogging the glass for a few seconds and obscuring my view.

"Isaac do you wan..." Ferron's voice trailed off.

I swung around to face him, schooling my face. "What is it, little man?" I kept my voice even.

His brow became marred with deep furrows, his hands shaking, but he continued to meet my gaze. "I... you... I've got cookies." He sounded breathless, as if he'd just been running a race rather than walking the few yards from the kitchen into the living room.

Had he picked up on my tension?

I sighed as I eyed his stiff posture. I'd noticed that since we'd talked about him no longer finding the joy in submission, he no longer went into a submissive pose. My heart rejoiced at the fact that he could act more naturally around me.

Did he do the same with Mark? The question popped into my head as I recalled how I'd insisted on Mark visiting the night before. He'd been only too happy to come and check on Ferron after his missed appointment due to what had happened.

They'd spent two hours in back room I hardly used

while I'd struggled to settle in another room. When I'd found myself tempted to eavesdrop on the conversation, I'd gone for a walk instead. When I'd returned Ferron had refused to come out of his room, Mark's grim expression as he said goodbye leaving me feeling even edgier.

Ferron hopped from one foot to the other in the doorway as if he couldn't quite decide what he should do next, making me realise I hadn't answered him. "Cookies would be good with a cuppa to go with them. And then maybe we could sit and have a chat?"

His chin wobbled, his eyes sheening with tears. But he nodded, swinging around to walk back into the kitchen with his shoulders slumped.

My brows pinched together. Was it time to push for answers? Nathan had given me some details about the state Ferron had been in when he'd arrived at his apartment. But he'd not been able to fill me in on any other details. Could I push him? Or was he still too fragile after everything that had happened?

Stop making excuses and man up.

He can tell you where to go if he's not interested.

That thought was scarier than facing ten armed men with nothing but my mind. I was fucking doomed!

Chapter Four

Ferron

I'd delayed the inevitable for as long as I could, making the tea just the way Isaac liked it and setting the tray carefully. Picking it up, I sucked in a shaky breath praying that I could be brave. That I could do as Mark had suggested the night before and talk to Isaac.

That's why I'd gone into the kitchen this morning, Isaac failing to hide his disappointment when I hadn't been able to give the police anything valuable. The policemen had been kind, but they'd clearly felt that I was wasting their time. And they were right; I had been.

Mark had laid it all out for me. Pointing out that if I didn't fully face up to what had happened, I'd never be able to let go of the fear and dread of one day ending up back in that room held against my will, doing...

I left the thought unfinished, not wanting to recall what had happened, given the vivid nightmares I'd been having. A part of me was grateful that I hadn't screamed at the top of my lungs and alerted Isaac to my distress. Whereas the other part had wanted to be held, to be protected from the boogie man who hid in my dreams waiting to come back to life.

Those men were still out there and they wanted me. Now I needed to decide whether I was going to continue to stay hidden and cower for the rest of my life, or stand up and fight to take back what those men had taken from me.

Talking it through with Mark was scary, but I felt braver each time I managed to let out a little more of what had happened between myself and Devon. It was almost like I was a pressure cooker letting off steam. I just wasn't sure if releasing it all at once would make things better or worse. I had a feeling it would probably be the latter and that was the reason why I'd told Mark that I'd need to think it through.

How did that work out for you?

My jaw ached, memories of Devon's torture burning behind my closed eyelids as I tried to block them out. The sounds of movement coming from the living room enabled me to shove the images away. *You can do this.* If there was a lack of conviction inside my head, I chose to ignore it as I stood a little straighter. My knuckles whitened as I clasped the tray tighter.

Isaac is your happy place, he'll help you.

With the thought running through my head on

repeat, I walked unsteadily into the lounge. My gaze swept the room landing on Isaac's stiff back as he stared out of the window, not turning around as I entered. Nervously chewing my lower lip between my teeth, I placed the tray on the table, the mugs rattling. I eyed them and gave a relieved sigh when the tea didn't spill.

A quick glance towards Isaac revealed that he hadn't moved. *Please look at me*, I silently begged, uncertain how to start a conversation with him when he had his back to me.

The seconds seemed to drag as I sat on the big sofa in front of the coffee table, lifting a mug and hoping it would warm my icy hands. After I'd taken several sips of the sweet tea, Isaac finally turned to face me, his expression unreadable. By the time he came over to take his mug and sit on the armchair facing the sofa, my chest felt as if I was trying to squeeze it into a top five times too small.

I chanced a look at him from beneath my eyelashes, wishing I hadn't when I saw sadness shadow his eyes.

"I'm not going to try and force you to talk about stuff that's clearly painful for you, little man. But I want you to know that when you're ready I'm here for you."

His quiet tone held a wealth of emotion that forced me to swallow and blink back the sudden tears that wanted to escape. His gaze shifted to somewhere just above my head, my heart dropping. What was that about? Why wouldn't he look at me?

"I want you to know that what I'm about to say is not about putting pressure on you, it's about me being honest with you and myself." He took a gulp of tea, his Adam's apple bobbing while his gaze was still fixed elsewhere.

Was he anxious?

I watched Isaac more closely, noting the way his leg was bouncing and the fingers of the hand on the chair arm moved restlessly over the fabric. He *was* anxious. But why? Almost as if he'd read my thoughts, his leg stopped moving and his hand stilled.

"You'll need to bear with me while I try to explain some... stuff." He took another drink of his tea. "You know I can still remember how you looked the first time I saw you. You had on a black shirt and fitted jeans. Your hair was a little longer than it is now, but it was your eyes that captured my attention. They held a wealth of sadness, but underneath it there was a spirited soul that... that called to me."

Given the soft way he was speaking, it took a second to register what he'd said. I froze with the mug halfway to my lips, my mouth hanging open. What did he mean that I'd "called to him?" But before I could gather my wits about me enough to question it, he'd already carried on as if he was oblivious to the fact that he was rocking my world.

"I haven't talked about the way I spectacularly outed myself about what I was into on the day you first moved in. I want to believe it was because I was too chicken shit, but I'd be lying. I've never hidden who I am, little man, not from anyone. But the Daddy side of my nature kinda never came up before because I've never found a boy I wanted enough to call my own... not until you."

He exhaled so noisily as he finished talking that I had to go over it in my head twice before I could figure out the meaning behind his words. *Until me.* Had he really meant that? At least it answered the question of whether he'd ever had a boy before. If I believed him anyway.

Why wouldn't you? When has Isaac ever lied to you?

Never. In all the time I'd spent with him, at home and at work, and hell, even before that, he'd never shown himself to be anything less than truthful. These revelations didn't leave me anywhere to hide though. Had I always known he felt this way?

I wanted to shake it off as absurd, but memories of how I'd always felt around him started to surface, memories that I couldn't disregard that easily. Had my heart known all along and I'd ignored it? Had those inner trembles been my heart's way of showing me what I wanted? Had I used my stupid infatuation with Carl to shield my heart? When I couldn't come up with an obvious answer and all I had were more questions, I sighed.

It was only as Isaac's face shuttered that I realised he might have taken my sigh to mean that I wasn't interested. *Shit, shit!*

I plonked the mug back onto the tray the remaining tea sloshing over the edge in my haste to stand. "I... I..." I yanked on my hair. My whole body was taut with tension which prevented me from being able to get the words out. My eyes started to ache.

Isaac got up slower, reaching around me to place his mug down. He didn't appear to know what to do with his hands as he stood and faced me, his fingers eventually curling into a ball at his sides. The vulnerability in his eyes stole my breath away and allowed me to consider stepping around the barrier I hid behind for the first time in ages.

The one step that separated us felt as wide as The Grand Canyon, but I took it anyway knowing what I'd get at the end of it. The second my body pressed against Isaac's, his scent surrounded me. I wrapped my arms around his waist and buried my head in his solid chest. His body tensed for a moment, but then his arms slid around me. Only then did I release the breath which had been trapped in my lungs. A shudder rippled through me at the feel of his chin resting on the top of my head.

"I could have lost you again," he whispered, his voice thick with emotion.

I knew what he meant, my arms holding him tighter. Keeping my face buried in his T-shirt, I licked my lips. "I... I think I need to tell you some things... then, if you still want to try..." I couldn't finish the sentence because I couldn't even contemplate what it would do to me if he chose to push me away.

"Look at me." He shifted back, lifting his hands to cup my cheeks as his gaze met mine. His voice was filled with steely determination as he spoke. "There is nothing you could say that would change what I *feel*, or what I *want* from you."

At the emphasis he put on some of his words, my heart stuttered. How could he say that when he didn't know what I'd done to survive? When he didn't know how tainted I was?

Chapter Five

Isaac

I struggled to keep control as a look of defeat crossed Ferron's face and he pulled away from me. It hurt my heart to let him go, but he needed to tell me what was on his mind on his own terms. The promise I'd made lay heavy as he went back over to the sofa and sat down looking lost. When he took a sip of what had to be tepid tea, I cringed.

"Do you want me to make another pot or freshen that cup?"

His chuckle was humourless as he shook his head. "This is fine." He sighed as he looked at the mug and then back to me. "Can you sit down? You're making me nervous standing over me."

Although asking for what he wanted put a certain

amount of trepidation in his voice, I didn't sense any fear. When we'd returned from the hospital I'd feared that he might slip back into old habits when it came to asking for something. But the moment he'd stepped inside my home, it was as if he'd felt... safe. Was it my house, or was it me that gave him that feeling?

I shook off the thought, concentrating on the small victories he'd achieved instead and hoping that I'd helped in some way. I prayed that I'd have enough courage to be what he needed when he did talk because the tension in his body spoke volumes. Needing to touch him, needing to be close to him, I asked tentatively, "can I sit next to you?"

"Yeah, I'd like that."

His meek reply did crazy things to my heart as I sat, twisting my body around so that I could face him. He took two big shuddery breaths, his fingers turning white around the mug as he stared into it like it held all the answers. "I'm gonna start with something I maybe should have mentioned from the start... Devon was never my boyfriend." He licked his lips, giving me a quick glance before focusing his gaze back on the mug.

I bit my tongue to stop myself from asking how that could be possible when they'd been living together. Laying the palms of my hands flat against my thighs, I exhaled slowly and waited. I didn't have to wait that long.

"You know I had an... infatuation with Carl? It wasn't a secret that I mooned after him. Anyway, after making a fool of myself I decided to try and find a new BDSM club. I needed a break from The Playroom." He shrugged nonchalantly, but there was so much pain in his voice that I had to reach out and touch him, to soothe some of the hurt even if I didn't fully understand it. Resting my hand on his thigh, I squeezed gently. He didn't acknowledge my touch, as if he was so lost in the past that he hadn't felt it.

"Wren asked around for me and he gave me the address of the Dom's Haven. I filled out the form, not realising what the questions were all geared towards. Then I went for my first visit. When they took my phone, keys and credit card I thought it was odd. But in my excitement, I didn't question it." His hands shook as he paused briefly to take another sip of cold tea. I wanted to tell him to stop, my belly quivering and a buzzing starting up in my head.

"It was only when one of the Doms took me to the manager's office that things started to freak me out. But by then it was too late."

His voice was barely louder than a whisper, his arms starting to tremble. Silent tears rolled down his cheeks as he finally lifted his head to look at me. What I saw in the depths of his gaze stabbed at me more effectively than any knife could. Being met with such utter devastation and blind terror cut me so deep that I wasn't sure I'd ever recover. I took the mug from his icy fingers and all but threw it onto the tray. The need to console him was all I could think about as one question pounded at my skull. What had they done to my precious boy?

I pulled him into my lap and he curled into me, his

hands gripping my T-shirt and clinging to it as if he was about to fall. Tears dripped from his quivering chin as he continued on with his story. "They gave me to Devon... They gave me to him without even asking if it was what I wanted. Not once did anyone ask me what I wanted. He took me... ohmygod! He... took... me... to... hell," he cried in anguish as his face pressed into my chest, the inconsolable weeping hacking at my defences.

What did he mean they gave him to Devon?

My brain was still trying to compute what he'd meant, the buzzing in my skull now sounding more like a swarm of angry bees. I couldn't think for a moment. *Taken?* Had he been *kidnapped*?

The wave of terror accompanying the thought lodged what felt like a tennis ball in my throat, making it impossible to swallow or to breathe. Sweat gathered at my temples and I fought to keep my hold gentle as realisation after realisation slammed into me.

All the pieces of the jigsaw puzzle fell into one hideous, gut-wrenching picture: Ferron's reactions, the way he wouldn't speak about Devon, the grim look on Mark's face last night. It all made sense now. My arms went lax as another thought registered. Was what had happened in the street somehow connected to the club, to what had happened between Devon and Ferron? Did this mean that Ferron wasn't safe even with Devon behind bars?

"Ferron, Ferron, look at me please," I begged, my voice rasping with my throat so dry. He lifted his tear-drenched face, his swollen, red-rimmed eyes not quite meeting my gaze. My insides turned to jelly. "Did the incident in the street have something to do with the Dom's Haven?"

His eyes flooded with fresh tears and my heart sank even before he nodded. He hiccupped past a sob, scrubbing at his wet cheeks, "I'm sorr—"

"Don't you dare apologise for what those bastards did to you," I ground out through clenched teeth, struggling to keep my temper on a short leash.

He looked dejected, his entire body tensing and shifting away from me.

"Fuck! Fuck, I'm sorry. I'm not cross at you, I swear, little man." I found myself tensing as he gave another sob followed by several hiccups. Then his body went slack against me.

I breathed in deeply, letting the feeling of air filling my chest to capacity settle me. Or at least I tried to convince myself it had, because in reality I wasn't sure anything would allow me to be calm ever again, not until I knew that every one of the fuckers had paid for whatever they'd done to my boy!

Only once I had some semblance of control did I cup his cheeks again and get him to look at me. "I want you to know that this is not your fault—"

"Yes, it is. Not all of it, no. But, the stuff..." he hiccupped and sniffed "...that Devon did to me, that I did to survive... that wasn't my fault. But going to that club without properly looking into it, that's on me and no one else," he said, snivelling.

"What I did to survive." That phrase made my heart

roll in my chest, tearing at my self-control. His eyes implored me not to argue with him. I didn't want to; I wanted...

The thought hung there, my heart squeezing with anguish. Did I want the whole story at the moment? Could I cope with more? My stomach revolted with the urge to vomit. I closed my eyes and took three steadying breaths.

When I opened them and met Ferron's distressed gaze, I could see he was at the end of his tether. There were lines of exhaustion around his eyes and I wasn't sure how much more either of us could take. I knew for damn sure that my heart, and my soul, wasn't ready to cope with what was surely only the tip of a very deep iceberg. There was also the fact that I was struggling to keep my distress hidden.

I was already undergoing an epic battle with what I'd found out so far taking its toll. My body felt like I'd gone ten rounds in the boxing ring with Nathan without dodging even one punch. If I went an extra round, I wasn't sure I'd be able to give Ferron what he needed because I sure as hell knew he'd endured more than beatings.

Had he been raped?

Motherfucker! Not now. Don't think about it.

Bile rose burning the back of my throat. I willed the tea working its way back up my oesophagus to stay put. Only after I'd swallowed twice did I feel able to speak. "We'll agree to disagree for now. What I'd like, if you'll let me, is to just sit here and hold you? Is that okay?" I cursed the thickness of my voice.

"I'm okay with that... if... Daddy wants to hold me."

His eyelashes fluttered closed to conceal his eyes, but not before I'd seen the fear of rejection in them. Then there was his hesitancy over the use of the word, Daddy. He slashed at my battered heart like a man with a machete.

Oh fuck, how could love hurt so much, yet be such a joy at the same time?

My jaw was throbbing by the time I had my emotions back under control. "That's right, little man, Daddy's going to take care of you now and for as long as you want."

If I secretly sent up a silent prayer that that would be forever, it wasn't hurting anyone else but me, right?

Chapter Six

Ferron

The groggy feeling I always got from sleeping during the day lingered as I sat wrapped in Isaac's embrace and listening to him breathe. The slow rhythm suggested he was asleep so I kept still, not wanting to disturb him.

You're trying to hide again.

Give me a break.

Do you think you deserve one? Do you think you deserve anything? Devon's voice took over despite me doing my best to quell it.

Would I ever be able to shut the fucker out?

Happy place, happy place!

Inhaling Isaac's scent, I snuggled into him, closing my eyes and focusing on what I knew for a fact was my safe place. I'd felt it the moment we'd walked into his home after what had happened in London. It was as if I'd shed a heavy blanket as he'd shut the door behind us. Mark had said that was a good thing, but had warned me that I'd need to find other places that made me feel safe as well.

The thing was, I didn't think I wanted to, not with Isaac's confession about wanting me for all those years still warming me from the inside out. Was what I was feeling real? Or was I doing what I'd always done? Latching onto someone that had shown they wanted me?

I wasn't sure what to think, what to feel. But Isaac's emotions when he'd spoken about his feelings had seemed real enough. Could someone fake that depth of emotion? What about movie stars?

Oh, shut up!

He has feelings for me, he does!

You have them for him too. You want him to take care of you.

It was true, I did. Calling him Daddy gave me butterflies in the pit of my stomach, but in a good way. Surely, that had to count for something? I huffed out a frustrated breath, continuing to go around in circles. A few hours of sleep clearly wasn't enough time to be able to process my true feelings. I had bucketloads of feelings. I just needed more time to sort through them and decide what to do about them.

You picked him as your happy place for a reason. Stop second guessing yourself. Look what happened last time!

I tensed, doing my best to shut out the reminder.

"You're a noisy thinker," Isaac said sleepily as he nuzzled my head.

My pulse skipped several beats as his lips brushed my hair.

"What time is it?"

I squinted at the small clock on the shelf under the TV. "It's just after three. You must be getting hungry. You missed lunch and didn't eat any of my cookies."

Isaac paused in the process of kissing my head, the action enough to make me go over what I'd just said. *Shit!* Why had I mentioned missing a meal? Mentally slapping myself, I waited to see what he'd say.

"Yeah, I'm hungry. What about we make a meal together? Then... maybe we could talk some more," he mumbled into my hair.

I tensed.

You can do this. If you can survive Devon, you can do this!

My heart beat rapidly against my ribs as the thought registered. I'd never considered it that way before and it put a different slant on everything. I had survived! Not only that but I'd found a man who wanted me, who wanted to be my special someone. Tears burned my throat and I sniffed willing them to go away. Unable to talk past the constriction in my throat, I simply nodded.

I let his body heat wrap around me like a security blanket for a few extra seconds before I climbed off his lap. The stiffness in my legs and back made me resemble a baby giraffe trying to walk for the first time. Heat flooded my face as Isaac chuckled. I blew out a noisy breath, my fringe lifting as I arched my brow. "You wouldn't be laughing at me, would you?"

Isaac's eyes gleamed with amusement. "Who me? Nah." A grin spread across his face as he got up off the sofa and stretched his arms up to the ceiling. His crumpled T-shirt rode up to reveal a strip of hairy skin.

My eyes widened at the nice tingly feeling in my groin. Oh bugger! Feeling flustered, I spun around and grabbed blindly for the tray needing to occupy my hands before I did something utterly stupid like reach out and touch that furry skin. A shiver rippled down my body, the stuff on the tray rattling.

Isaac shifted behind me, as if he could tell the impact he was having on me. The heat and scent of him was tantalisingly close, but he wasn't close enough to actually touch me.

His mouth brushed my ear. "You alright, little man?"

"I'm fine," I croaked out, giving a good attempt at mimicking a frog as yet more heat filled my cheeks. At this rate, I'd be brighter than a bloody lighthouse beacon. A sigh escaped before I could stop it. Isaac's hot breath ghosted my cheek for a second before it disappeared.

Breathing a little easier, I walked in the direction of the kitchen, refusing to look back as I heard Isaac's heavy footsteps behind me. Once I was in the kitchen, I placed the tray down and went over to the fridge to see what I could use to make a meal.

With my head in the fridge, I called out what we had. "There's chicken breasts, lamb chops or there's mince that I could use to make either lasagne or a pasta sauce." Isaac was a big meat eater and would have it for every meal if he could.

"The lasagne, because at least I can help with that."

I pulled the packet of mince out of the fridge and closed the door before widening my eyes in alarm at Isaac. "How so? The last time you *helped*, you got distracted by something on your phone and burnt the sauce." The easy banter felt good after the morning's confession and I held onto it, aware that it wouldn't last once I got to the crux of what had happened.

I went to grab the rest of the ingredients, pausing as Isaac stood in front of me with his hands on his waist.

"What? Is it my fault that you gave me the most boring job?" he scoffed, his eyes gleaming with mirth.

"Yeah, yeah, don't forget that you could set fire to water. How I thought stirring a sauce was something you could manage is beyond me." I sighed for dramatic effect, laying the back of my hand against my forehead in the style of an actress from an old Fifties movie.

A giggle bubbled out as he gave me a mock glare.

"You wouldn't be mocking me, would you?" He tried for a sinister scowl but his eyes gave him away even before he burst out laughing and made a grab for me. I wasn't quick enough to evade him, his fingers finding the tickly spot right under my ribs. Before I knew it, I was hysterical laughter turning my limbs heavy and making it nigh on impossible to fight as I weakly tried to fend him off.

"Do you surrender?" Isaac asked through his laughter, his fingers mercilessly carrying on.

"Yes, yes. I surrender," I gasped out. Choking, I flopped against him as he stopped tormenting me. My chest heaving, I wiped at my wet cheeks, registering how much they ached. God, it was good to laugh like that. My happiness was too much to contain and I gave Isaac a beaming smile wanting to share it with him.

He stilled for a few seconds before lifting his hands to gently cup my cheeks. There were so many different emotions flitting across his face that I struggled to grasp what they all meant.

"You are so beautiful when you smile." His thumbs grazed my cheekbones in the gentlest of caresses, his gaze bewitching me. "God, when you direct it at me. I want..." He trailed off on a shuddery breath.

"You want what?" I prompted him breathlessly, desperate for him to continue even as my thundering pulse made it difficult to breathe.

"You! Just you." He moaned as if he was in agony before dragging me closer to him and hoisting me off the ground.

Given the tension rolling off him, I expected a hard kiss, so I was surprised at the soft brush of his lips against mine. The caress was so sweet that it derailed my thoughts. Isaac's whole body seemed to vibrate as he held me captive with my feet still not touching the ground.

The only part of us touching were his hands under my arms and his lips against mine. Yet I felt the imprint of him against every part of me. Despite his tongue stroking against mine, he still kept the kiss gentle. The sweetness of the gesture did more to arouse me than anything I'd ever experienced before. It burned through me like a spark to dry wood. The desire that I'd assumed was long dead ignited again and I found my legs lifting to wrap around Isaac's waist.

The action somehow made the moment all the more real as his arousal pushed against... mine. *My cock is hard. My cock is hard!* Panic blindsided me and I wrenched my mouth from Isaac's, panting as I tried to pull in some air at the same time as wriggling to get down.

Isaac immediately lowered me to the floor, lifting his hands so I could see them as if he was trying to reassure me. But I was way too busy staring down at my groin to acknowledge the action. Holy fuck, I was still hard!

Chapter Seven

Isaac

A wave of dizziness swept through me as I struggled to keep it together. I knew better than to push so why had I kissed him? Why?

My jaw clenched as Ferron's gaze dipped. I held my hands in the air so he could see them. The last thing I wanted was him thinking I might lash out just because he'd... well, I wasn't sure what had happened.

It had been heaven enough just to be kissing him, but I'd nearly died on the spot when he'd willingly wrapped his legs around my waist. Then something had set him off. A bad memory, maybe? Had I been too aggressive? *Fuck, could it be that?*

I ran my hands through my hair forgetting for a moment that I'd intended on leaving them where Ferron could see them. I was so busy having a private meltdown that the fact he hadn't flinched didn't register for several seconds. In fact, he hadn't appeared to notice anything. What had I missed?

I shook my head, hoping to clear the equal amounts of desire and panic caused by Ferron's reaction. My gaze swept over him. But then his head rose and I shifted my gaze to meet his.

There was wonderment in his eyes and something else I couldn't interpret. His chin wobbled and I exhaled noisily when, instead of the tears I'd expected, he gave me a smile that could have rivalled the sun for brightness. "I'm hard! My cock is hard!"

His voice was filled with such excitement and wonder. But all I felt was confusion, quickly followed by a dread which twisted my stomach into knots.

"I didn't think it would happen. I mean, before I didn't want it to, but then I got away and I just thought it was something that wouldn't come back, you know, after what he'd done. But look! I'm hard." He jabbered the words so fast that they all ran into each other but I could still build a picture of why this moment was so momentous to him.

Black spots formed in front of my eyes as air refused to enter my lungs. *That fucking bastard. I will kill him.*

The bite of my fingernails in my palms barely stopped the cry of anguish which choked me. I'd bet my last pound that Ferron had no idea what he'd just revealed in his excitement. *Fucking, shitting hell!*

I wanted more than anything to be able to celebrate

with him, but all I could think about was what he must have suffered to stop him from feeling any arousal.

Push it aside for now. Come on, he needs you.

I forced my mouth into what I hoped was a sexy grin as I opened my arms. "Do you want to show, Daddy?"

There was still excitement in his expression but his lips pinched together as he nodded. The two steps he needed to take to move into my embrace seemed to take forever, and only once he was pressed against me did I release my tense muscles.

He snuggled into me for a moment before allowing his lower body to come into contact with my thigh. Although he wasn't as firm as he'd been when he'd pushed against me while we'd kissed, he was still aroused enough for it to be noticeable.

Relinquishing control to him, I kept my body relaxed as I stroked up and down his back. First came a soft sigh, then a little moan before he wriggled closer pressing himself more firmly against me. After long, torturous minutes of him rubbing himself against me, he pulled back far enough for me to be able to see his flushed face. "Thank you, Daddy."

His earnest expression made my jaw clench with the need, the want, to devour him greedily. *He's not ready. You're not ready.*

I used the thought as a mantra as I lay a soft kiss on his mouth. The dreamy sigh that followed was a balm to my soul as I lifted my head and flicked a finger down his nose. "You're welcome, little man. Whatever you need from Daddy, I'll give it to you, okay?"

His long eyelashes fluttered for a second, his cheeks turning a deep red as he gave me a shy smile. "Can I have another kiss before I make the lasagne?" The lines around his mouth gave away his anxiety.

Moving slowly so that he understood my intention, I lowered my mouth to his. I hovered there for a second letting the sexual tension build. Only when he gave a needy moan did I press my mouth to his. The sweet taste of him flooded my mouth as he parted his lips and I swept my tongue into his mouth. He mewled as my tongue stroked along his. I kept the caress light and teasing.

When he pulled back gasping and flushed, it took every ounce of willpower I had to stop myself from dragging him back in for another taste.

"Daddy... you're really good at that. I think my toes are melting."

I winked at him as he giggled. "Maybe we need to do it again so I can see if I can melt any other part of you."

"You melted me from top to toe. I'm lucky I can still stand," he accused while trying to contain his giggles.

I waggled my eyebrows at him. "That was my dastardly plan all along."

He rolled his eyes at me. "Then who would cook your meals?" he asked playfully. He gave a big smirk before going over to the counter with a bounce in his step.

A part of me wanted to keep the light-hearted banter going, but after what he'd said earlier there was no way I'd be able to settle until I knew everything. I was done hiding. I just hoped I had the strength to give my boy everything he needed.

"Do you want a glass of wine?" I asked, keeping my tone neutral. If I hadn't been watching him closely, I might have missed the way his hand trembled for a second as he picked up the packet of mince.

"Yeah, that would be lovely."

His voice was strained and I had the overwhelming urge to stop the conversation, my protective feelings showing themselves at the slightest sign of his distress. I pushed them away knowing it wouldn't do either of us any good if I had no idea how to navigate a relationship with someone who'd suffered past trauma.

After checking the fridge and finding no wine, I went to grab a bottle from the garage. By the time I got back, the kitchen was filled with the scent of cooking meat, onions and garlic. My stomach gurgled in appreciation as I strolled over to the counter to grab a couple of glasses.

Once the wine was open, I poured two glasses, leaving one by Ferron's hand. I didn't say anything as I took my own glass and went to sit on one of the kitchen chairs closest to him.

After a few swallows with the alcohol buzzing through me pleasantly, I licked my dry lips. "Can you tell me what happened after the men gave you to Devon?"

Chapter Eight

Ferron

There was no way of pretending I hadn't heard the question that had been asked. Besides, I was pretty sure Isaac had spotted the way I'd tensed. And it wasn't like I hadn't been expecting this after we'd set off down the path earlier. But was it so wrong to want to cling a little longer to the sexy moment which had made me feel... normal?

Normal, what did that even mean?

Fuck knows, because what did it matter when this was what counted? Acknowledging that made me swing around to face Isaac. I needed to face this, face *him*, if I wanted what would come next. I had to make this count, for both of us.

I rubbed my hands together as I met his steady gaze. At the warmth in the depths of his eyes, I released a gusty exhale. "Devon locked me up in his home for over a year," I rushed to say on one big breath. So much so that I ended up panting and having to stop for a second to draw in another breath. Isaac's face was an unreadable mask, making it difficult to decide whether I should keep going.

Get it over with!

"He held me prisoner and made me... do... stuff... to him. He punished me every day until all there was... was pain. Until I believed that was all I could ever expect from life because I was worthless. That if I tried to escape... I'd be less than worthless without him."

I wasn't aware I was crying until Isaac shot off the chair so quickly that he was almost a blur. He lifted me again, but this time held me more like a baby. He rocked me in his arms as the pain ripped through me leaving my wounds exposed and bleeding. Sobs tore from my throat and with them came the emotions I'd held on to so tightly. The release was so profound that my screams rent the air. Once they'd started, I couldn't seem to stop even though my throat and chest burned. They continued to pour out of me as if my body was purging itself. Wave upon wave of dizziness rolled through me and I was no longer sure if the motion I felt was due to Isaac rocking me, or if it was me moving. It didn't seem to matter when I sounded like an animal being tortured.

I turned my face into Isaac's solid chest trying to muffle the sounds. Yet, they still seemed to fill my head. My eyes were throbbing so I squeezed them shut. Nothing seemed to keep the chill from invading my limbs. Shudders wracked my body despite the heat rolling off Isaac.

Then my body touched a soft surface and I struggled to open my eyes in order to figure out what was happening. Isaac's bedroom came into focus as he pulled the duvet over me, wrapping his large body around mine on the mattress. I forced myself to focus on the heat and the familiar scent using it to soothe my battered soul.

Through the misery, a thought registered. I tried to move but Isaac was holding on to me too tightly. "The... food," I rasped out through my raw throat, the pain making it impossible to speak any louder than a mere whisper.

"I've switched off the cooker. We'll order something later." His voice was so deep that I struggled to grasp what he'd said. I got the gist though so I closed my eyes and let him hold me. I let him protect me from the past, from what still needed to be talked about.

He lifted his hand to gently stroke my hair. "I'm sorry, little man, I'm so very sorry." Even with his voice thick with emotion, his touch remained gentle.

"I am too... I am too," I said between sobs. "But being sorry doesn't change anything."

His body tensed for a moment before the stroking resumed. "The past can't be changed, little man, you're right. But see, this moment right here, can make all the difference. The past is gone, if not forgotten. But we can build something solid that will help to heal those wounds inside you. The scars show that you survived. The strength, the courage it takes to get up every day and carry on is what defines you. The moment you chose to survive shows me your true strength and your courage," he whispered, utter conviction filling his voice.

His lips brushed the top of my head as the words sank past the despair, somehow making the ache inside me a little less painful.

Was I strong?

The weariness and exhaustion I felt after what I'd just done said otherwise. If anything, I felt weaker for not being able to stop the breakdown from happening. Yet with Isaac holding me, I wanted what he'd said to be true, not only for him but for me too.

"Stop thinking about it, little man. Rest. I'll be here when you wake up. I'll keep you safe."

Taking him at his word, I let the exhaustion drag me into the darkness.

"Do you want to talk about what's on your mind? You've been sat staring out of the patio door for the last ten minutes whilst chewing your lip. At this rate, I'm not sure there's going to be anything left of it," Mark said, chuckling.

When I shifted my gaze to him though, his brow was furrowed and there were deep creases around his eyes. "I do, but I'm worried I'll... I'll start screaming."

Mark's brows moved so far up his forehead that I thought they were going to merge with his receding hair-line. I quickly rushed to explain. "Isaac and I had a talk like you suggested. Only once I told him about Devon holding me prisoner, I kind of lost it." I shifted uncomfortably on the leather seat. That was a little bit of an understatement, but whatever. It had been nearly a week since it had happened and Isaac hadn't pushed me to say more. Although I was grateful, I felt like he was waiting for the other shoe to drop. He had every right to feel like that because what came next was...

Leave it alone. Face it when you need to.

It was draining to continually hold the horror inside. It made me feel like I was constantly wading through thick mud.

"It was bound to happen at some point, Ferron. I'm glad it has. Even though you've cried in here, you've continued to keep some of your emotions in check." Mark leaned forward, his expression serious. "I'm sure that's because of what Devon did to you. It would have been the one thing you had control over. It's probably scary right now as you try and work through all those previously blocked emotions. Now that you've broken through the barrier, it will initially be harder to control yourself, which can I just add is not necessarily a bad thing." His head tilted to one side and he got that look that signified that I needed to listen without arguing.

I gave a wry chuckle and nodded. "Alright, I'll try and go with it." That was all I could promise because I didn't like the idea that I might have a meltdown in front of my friends or work colleagues, never mind doing it again in front of Isaac. I shuddered at the very idea.

"When did you have the talk with Isaac? And how

did you feel about it afterwards?" The matter of fact way Mark spoke eased the knots in my stomach and I found myself explaining what had happened. By the end of the session I was drained, but I was more hopeful than I'd been going into his office.

Maybe I wasn't a freak after all?

Or maybe...

The second I registered Devon's insidious voice slipping into my mind, I shut the thought down. Happy place, happy place! Goddamnit, happy bloody place!

Chapter Nine

Isaac

The last six days had been like walking on broken eggshells. The need to have Ferron in my sight at all times hadn't abated, not even a little. It warred with the need to find the fuckers that had hurt my boy and rip them apart. With Ferron always within earshot, I hadn't had any opportunity to talk to anyone so I'd used his planned appointment with Mark today to get a couple of hours to myself.

As the door of the car slammed shut and the engine started up, I waved at Ferron and gave Nathan a nod. He reversed out onto the road and drove off. The knot in my belly was ignored as I closed the door and pulled my phone out to search the contact list before hitting dial. I only had to wait a couple of seconds before it was answered.

"Yo, is it clear?" came the deep baritone voice on the other end of the phone.

"Yeah, the front door is open, just come in." I didn't get a response but then I hadn't expected one. Joshua was a man of few words. But action was a different story.

When I'd asked Nathan to take Ferron to his appointment, he hadn't questioned it. Ferron though had gone around all morning with his face tripping him up. I'd had to bite my tongue more than once to stop myself from saying that I'd changed my mind. Thankfully, my feeling of uselessness that I hadn't been able to change what had happened in the past had kept me silent. The need to make sure that Ferron remained safe was my top priority now, and if my heart ached when he was away from me, then so be it.

At the sound of my front door opening, I shook off my worries and pasted a smile on my face.

The second, Joshua Devlin, or Phoenix to those who really knew him, Nix for short, strolled in looking larger than life, my smile warmed. His dark blond hair was cropped to his skull making it hard to see the silver that was threaded through it when he left it to grow. His beard was trimmed close to his face and framed his full lips. The sparkle of devilment in his eyes was something which often surprised me, given my knowledge of some of the jobs he'd done in the past.

My eyes narrowed on his uncovered neck and in particular on the colourful tattoos creeping up it. The man was addicted to getting tattoos making me wonder how far he'd go with covering his body.

"What?" His blond brows met in the middle.

"You got more tattoos, didn't ya?" I said, chuckling as he shrugged his massive shoulders as if to say "and your point is?"

"My body is an artist's wet dream, what can I say." He glanced around the room. "You've got someone living with you."

Momentarily taken aback by the change of subject, I glanced around the room trying to see what was different since the last time Nix had been in my home. I shook my head and stared at him. "Why do you say that?"

"The feel of the place is more homely. There's a book on the table which is not your usual read. There's a throw blanket on the back of your sofa. There are several new plants and there are candles on the window ledge. You want me to go on?" His brows wagged at me as a smile lit up his face.

"Oh, fuck off, arsehole," I grumbled good-naturedly. "I didn't ask you to come here to point out the changes in my home."

"It's about time you took on a *boy*."

The way he stressed the last part made me roll my eyes. The fucker missed nothing and as annoying as it could be, it was the reason I'd called him. We'd trained together in the Navy and he'd become one of my most trusted friends. We'd kept in touch afterwards and given his recent move to London, along with the work he did for a security firm, I'd hoped he'd be able to help me find information on the Dom's Haven.

"Thanks." I sighed. "That's partly why I rang you. But before we get into it, do you want a drink?"

"Yeah, but don't go making that weak shit."

I gave him a two fingered salute before heading into the kitchen. Once he had a mug of coffee that he could have stood a spoon up in, we sat on the kitchen chairs facing each other across the table.

"Okay, lay it out for me." He took a sip of his coffee, eyeing me intently over the rim of the mug.

"Ferron is, or was, a sub at The Playroom. He joined about three years ago. About a year ago he embarrassed himself in The Playroom and had another club recommended to him. He didn't do any checks on the new place and blindly went off on his own. That's when things turned to shit. He was given to a Dom as a slave, locked in the fucker's home and forced to..." I sucked in a shaky breath, releasing it slowly.

Nix's eyes were no longer sparkling with devilment, but instead held a fierce light that I'd seen many times before. His mouth was drawn into a tight line.

"I'm sure you can imagine what happened. He managed to get away, but the Dom caught up with him on New Year's Eve. Only this time he took the owner of The Playroom's boyfriend, Lenny, as well. He held them both captive in the cellar at the club."

"I saw that on the news. Didn't they catch the guy, and isn't he in prison right now?" Nix asked, his brow furrowing.

"Yeah, he is. But a week ago some guy, a Dom, tried to snatch Ferron right off the fucking street. If I hadn't listened to my gut and followed him"—a shudder rippled through me—"fuck knows what could have happened. Anyway, it was only after that that Ferron started to open up about what had happened to him. I'm getting the impression that he was threatened so that he'd keep his mouth shut. Until recently, we'd all been under the impression that Devon was an arsehole ex who just wouldn't take no for an answer."

Needing to move, I stood up. "Believing that was bad enough, but this shit takes it to a whole new level." I stared at Nix. "This whole thing has my gut telling me that Ferron wasn't the first and that there are others suffering the same fate." I massaged my temples, hoping to ease the throbbing that the worry brought with it.

"What a fucking mess!" Nix declared as he stood too, his mug rattling against the wooden table, his six-foot-four frame seeming to vibrate with energy. His dark jacket strained around his bulging biceps and the combat style trousers he favoured did nothing to disguise the powerful body beneath. "What do you need from me? Whatever it is, it's yours."

Something released in my neck and back as he made the offer, a tension I hadn't even realised I'd been holding. "That's what I was hoping for. Now, do you think your security firm would be willing to take on a new client?"

Chapter Ten

Ferron

I chewed on my thumbnail as I eyed the colourful shirt that I'd bought the week before. When all the flamingo motif stuff had arrived for the new bar and restaurant above The Playroom I'd become a little fixated on it. I'd loved flamingos ever since the first time I'd seen them in a wildlife sanctuary.

Nathan's idea to name the club after my favourite bird had tickled me. So much so that when I'd come across the bold pink shirt with white flamingos on it while searching for a replacement pair of jeans after splashing bleach on the ones I wore to death, I'd one-clicked it faster than an Olympic swimmer diving into a pool.

Once it had arrived, I'd hidden it in the wardrobe like

a guilty pleasure, thinking I'd never get a chance to wear it. That was until I'd got a call from Lenny half an hour ago. Was it too much for Lenny's impromptu stag party for Adam? Apparently, Isaac had taken matters into his own hands after grumbling about Nathan's poor efforts at being a best man to his best friend and business partner, Carl. Even though our days off were usually spent together, I hadn't said anything about being left alone as Isaac had been acting a little odd lately. Ever since my last appointment with Mark, he'd been overprotective and had had a watchfulness about him that made me uneasy.

Once he'd left muttering something about Nathan being useless at being best man, I'd sulked in my bedroom for an hour at not being invited. Lenny had rung to tell me that they'd all left with Nathan and Carl in tow, the subs excluded from the day out. Not to be outdone, Lenny had decided to hold his own stag party for Adam, who worked with Lenny at the main restaurant, La Trattoria Di Amore.

The fact he'd invited me proved that he didn't hold a grudge for what had happened with Devon. He'd repeatedly said that there was nothing to forgive me for, but I'd always worried that he might just have been saying that to make me feel better. A smile spread across my face. Lenny really did like me. The smile faltered though as a thought occurred to me. How was I going to get to the apartment on the other side of London on my own? Cold sweat started to gather on my skin. Did I have enough to pay for an Uber?

I squinted as I tried to recall what was left in the new bank account I'd set up. I'd used all of my extra cash to pay back Nathan for the sessions with Mark which didn't leave me with a lot. *Shit!*

Tears gathered in my eyes and I willed them to go away. I could do this. I could get the train and the tube and go to a party like a normal person. A sob caught in my throat, my hands balling into fists.

I will do this.

With hands that trembled way more than I would have liked, I picked up the shirt and slipped it over my naked torso. It took several attempts to do up the buttons with my fingers so clumsy.

Once dressed, I checked myself out in the mirror, a smile spreading across my lips. The man staring back at me looked… happy. Regardless of Isaac's odd behaviour, he'd shown me daily how much he cared about me through little touches, like buying my favourite sweets and tucking me into bed at night with sweet kisses. My heartbeat picked up at the dreamy expression which had appeared on my face. When my groin heated too, I glanced away and quickly went in search of my wallet and keys.

By the time I'd reached the train station, I was convinced I was going to pass out. All my earlier confidence had fled, white splodges dancing in front of my eyes and the hairs on the back of my neck were standing on end. Twisting to look around for probably close to the hundredth time, I didn't see anyone I recognised though. It didn't make any difference to how I was feeling. In two minds whether I should just head back to Isaac's house, I shut my eyes and did one of Mark's breathing exercises.

Isaac believes in you. Isaac thinks you're strong.

I stopped the mantra when I heard a train approaching, feeling marginally better. I slowly opened my eyes and took another shaky inhale before stepping through the open door of the train.

Sitting in a seat close to the exit, I blew up the balloons, using the task to keep me occupied. My hands tightened around the bag despite the fact there was plenty of people as I exited the train. I couldn't help but remember when I'd shouted for help before and no one had done anything.

You're not worth helping, that's why.

"Fuck off Devon," I muttered under my breath, evidently not quietly enough though given the strange look I got from a guy walking past. I used the large bag of balloons as a barrier. People moved out of the way as I waved the huge sack in front of me. I did the same on the tube, standing by an exit with my back to the wall and the balloons in front of me. Although, what a large bag of bloody balloons was going to do to save me, God only knew.

By the time I got to Nathan's apartment I was a sweaty mess, but for the first time in a long time I felt proud of myself. I didn't have time to examine my feelings for long though, the door in front of me opening and Lenny grinning at me.

A little flustered, I began to rant. "If I never see another balloon again, it will be too soon. Who knew how much puff it took to blow up thirty fucking balloons? Never mind carry them on the..." All the blood in my body seemed to freeze as a huge guy I didn't recognise stepped out from behind the large counter which split the apartment into two.

"This is Bailey. He's Nathan's old sergeant," Lenny said in a rush as if he'd sensed my disquiet.

Bailey's smile was sweet and held an element of shyness that did a lot to ease the knots in my stomach. "I'm also a sub."

He was a sub?

Lenny's face was a picture as he tried to smother his laughter at my look of disbelief. Bailey was a huge man, which on the face of it screamed Dom not sub. But as I examined his posture there were certain traits that gave him away. I gave Bailey a small smile as I went over to the sofa to drop the sack on the cushion. There was a bark of laughter as I peeled off my coat.

"Oh, my God! Where the heck did you get that?" Lenny choked out past his laughter.

I turned to face him, a grin spreading across my face as I shrugged. "I might have had it in the back of my wardrobe."

"No way! You actually had that and didn't buy it as a gag?" His eyes widened incredulously as I nodded.

The sound of another knock stopped Lenny from saying more as he bounced on the spot for a second before rushing to the door. Soon the room was filled with laughter, all the anxiety I'd felt from travelling to the party gone.

As the afternoon wore on and I got sucked into the party spirit with a flurry of drinking games, Adam bet me that I couldn't get my head under the chocolate fountain while riding one of the large stuffed flamingos. The part of me that had never been able to resist a dare surfaced. At least that's what I blamed it on when I tried it half an hour later. Triumphant and covered in chocolate, I fell to the floor in a heap, laughing hysterically at both the state of me, and the flamingo. It looked like it had got into a mud fight with the other flamingos and lost.

Adam, his best friend Richie, Theo and Sawyer who were two waiters from the restaurant, as well as Bailey and Lenny all fell about laughing. The sound was glorious and I remembered what Isaac had said about the moments we make now being able to heal. He wasn't wrong. These men had given me back a part of my life I'd been missing—real friendship. My heart skipped a beat. What about Wren?

Through the haze of alcohol, the thought lingered as I lay on the floor. When was the last time I'd seen him at the club? Had he been coming to the club while I wasn't working? Was he still a member of The Playroom? I frowned up at the ceiling as it seemed to shift. The alcohol swimming around in my bloodstream made it hard to focus so I gave up.

I peeled open my gritty eyes to the sound of laughter, the ache in my arms telling me that I'd probably fallen asleep. Staggering to my feet, my eyes widened at the sight of the flamingo. Had I slept holding that thing all night? And what the heck was that all over it?

Nathan appeared from the hallway, heat filling my face as his gaze swept over me. His lips twitched, his eyes gleaming with humour. The incident with the chocolate fountain suddenly came back to me.

Oh crapola! Did Nathan think I was covered in shit? I ran my hand through my hair, only for it to get stuck in clumps of chocolate. I sighed mournfully.

Nathan stared at the couch and I noticed Bailey. His face was a shade of grey that would befit a corpse. My breath became trapped in my lungs as Nathan eyed the room. Lenny was in the kitchen, muttering as he frantically wiped at the sticky-looking mess which covered the marble worktops. He hadn't noticed Nathan yet.

"Can someone tell me what the hell happened here?" Nathan growled.

Lenny froze, his wild-eyed stare meeting Nathan's as his cheeks flamed. "Sir... I'm sorry. We had a stag party of our own. We got... a little... carried away," he stuttered, his gaze lowering but not before I'd seen a glint of humour in his eyes which allowed me to release the breath I held.

Nathan walked over to the counter. "Is something amusing you?"

Lenny's laughter was quickly followed by both Adam

and Richie's. Clutching the flamingo, I stood, working hard to suppress my own giggles.

My cheeks turned hot as Nathan gave Lenny a kiss.

Nathan turned to face the room. "Now, does someone want to explain why Ferron looks like he's covered in shit and my Serg looks like death warmed up?"

I couldn't contain my laughter any longer and it burst free.

Adam pointed at the table tucked away in the corner of the room. "Ferron thought he could stick his head under the fountain and drink the chocolate. Unfortunately, he was riding on the back of a flamingo while he was doing it." Adam grinned at me as he spoke.

"Hey, I think I remember you saying you'd give me fifty quid if I managed to do it?" I held my hand out, palm up and wriggled my fingers. "Pay up."

Richie just shook his head and carried on picking the crap up off the floor while Lenny chuckled.

Nathan pointed at me. "Those flamingos were more than fifty quid each so I think that money should be coming in my direction to pay for the replacements I'm going to need. No one is going to want a bloody flamingo that looks like it shat itself," Nathan said, grinning at me.

Had I fucked up? It took a second to see past the panic and register that his smile was genuine. In order to hide my alarm, I quipped, "What, you don't think customers would like a chocolate-coated flamingo? Don't you know it's the new craze?"

Nathan shook his head. "I'll give you a new bloody craze. It took me ages to source those stuffed animals."

Lenny slipped his arms around Nathan's waist and lay his head against his back. "It's alright, I'll have a look and see what I can do to replace them, seeing as it was my idea to use—"

Bailey sat up, looking bleary-eyed. "Stop... you know it was me that found them and brought them up here," he mumbled through his hands as he rubbed gingerly at his face. His bloodshot eyes demonstrated how much he'd had to drink as he slowly lowered his legs to the floor.

Once Bailey had headed to the bathroom and Richie had persuaded Lenny to make breakfast, I went in search of my phone. My stomach dropped as the screen lit up. Seventeen missed calls and fourteen text messages!

Crap, crappity, crap! I hadn't left Isaac a note to say where I'd gone.

I eyed the other men in the kitchen as I sucked my lower lip between my teeth. The fun I'd had was still fresh in my memory. *He didn't invite you to go with him yesterday.* I tried to justify my own behaviour, ignoring how whiney I sounded in my own head. *Oh, like that will work as an argument, he's a bloody Dom Daddy!*

Expecting fear to accompany the thought, I was surprised when there was nothing more than a low level of anxiety buzzing inside me. I blew out a noisy breath and walked over to the window, pressing the button to return Isaac's call.

Chapter Eleven

Isaac

At the sound of Ferron's ringtone, I darted out of the chair and grabbed my phone off the coffee table. I'd placed it there earlier to stop myself from throwing it across the room. Paying no attention to the jackhammer pounding at my temples, I hit the button to accept the call, my hand shaking. "Ferron—"

"I'm so sorry, Daddy. Please don't be cross. I fell asleep at Lenny's holding a flamingo because I'd had too much to drink at the party," Ferron garbled, the words running into each other in his rush to speak.

The sound of my own knuckles cracking as I gripped the phone alerted me to the fact that if I wasn't careful, I'd crush the bloody thing while I deciphered what he'd said. Lenny, party and flamingo were the main things I'd managed to grasp past the buzzing in my ears. I exhaled gustily. "I'm coming to collect you, little man, then we can talk about it," I rasped out.

There was the sound of a choked sob on the other end of the phone before he muttered, "yes, Daddy."

I dropped the phone to the floor as soon as I'd ended the call. I sank back onto the chair, my legs no longer willing to hold me up. *He's okay. He's okay.* Massaging my temples, I closed my eyes, letting the relief sink past the dread that had gripped me by the throat while I'd been waiting for him to come home.

When I'd got back after the stag party and found the house in darkness, I'd assumed, wrongly as it turned out, that Ferron had been asleep in bed. When I'd gone to check on him, it had taken a minute in my slightly drunken state to figure out that he wasn't there. I swallowed the bile threatening to burn a trail up the back of my throat at the memory of finding the bed cold and empty. A shudder rippled down my spine as I pushed aside the feelings of dismay which had lingered all night.

The alcohol I'd consumed had been no defence against my fear. Eventually I'd managed to pull a sensible thought out of my head, but only after I'd frantically called Ferron four times and sent three messages without getting a response. I'd contacted Nix, who'd assured me that one of the men hired to watch my home had seen Ferron leave the house under his own steam dressed as if he was going out.

I'd kicked myself for not considering that Ferron might leave the house willingly. Up to now, he'd made no effort to go out on his own and I'd have bet my last pound that he hadn't been ready to try.

Yeah, right. He was not only ready, but he went to a fucking party!

So did you! Stop being a dick, he's allowed to have a life.

He didn't tell me where he was going.

You went out and didn't invite him so what do you expect?

"For Fuck's sake!" I growled to the empty room, admitting that I wasn't going to win my own bloody argument. Inhaling the scent of stale alcohol as I got up, I headed for the stairs for a quick shower.

I only felt marginally better after the shower, but I did at least smell fresher as I headed out of the house. The blustery wind tugged at my jacket as I stopped to see if I could spot the man watching my home.

Since meeting with Nix, he'd liaised with his boss, who'd arranged men to watch my home twenty-four-seven. Before managing the bar for Nathan, the work I'd done had been lucrative due to carrying a high risk of coming home in a coffin. Therefore, with the money I'd saved and the inheritance from my father, I had a sizable nest egg. My father often accused me of holding every penny I had prisoner. Ferron had changed that. I'd spend every last penny on him if it kept him safe.

Seeing nothing out of the ordinary, the tension riding me eased. The security team watching my home were now on Ferron duty after I'd remedied my stupidity. *Why hadn't I thought to have a man watch Ferron too? Because you didn't think he'd go anywhere without you, that's why!*

Nix had told me that he'd set up a meeting for me

and his boss in the next couple of days to talk over what I needed, but for now wherever Ferron went one of the security team would go too. My heart fluttered at the thought of the conversation I'd need to have with Ferron. He needed to know that I took his safety seriously, that his life was more important than any other.

Once I was in the car, I put the radio on full blast, hoping to kill the thoughts racing through my head. When all it did was add to the pounding in my skull that rivalled a jackhammer hitting a pavement, I switched it off. Cursing under my breath for not taking the time to take a pain meds, I pulled into traffic.

By the time I'd battled the London traffic and got out of my car, I wanted to beg for mercy. Instead, I stomped over to the lift in the underground garage. At Nathan's door, I cricked my neck before lifting my hand to knock. It opened and as I met Ferron's worried expression, the world disappeared as my heart leapt with joy at the sight of him.

"I'm so sorry, Daddy. Please don't... punish me," he implored, his eyes swimming with tears.

Love overwhelmed me and cut me off at the knees. It made it impossible to speak so I scooped him up into my arms instead and crushed him to my chest, burying my face in his hair. "What the fuck!" I reared back at the feel of...

What the fuck was in his hair?

My gaze narrowed on the brown lumps before shifting lower to his shirt. I sniffed carefully. "Have you got... chocolate in your hair?"

Ferron's face flushed scarlet as raucous laughter came from behind him. He lay his forehead against my chest, trying to hide his face. "Yeah," he mumbled.

I shifted my gaze to the group of men in Nathan's apartment. "Someone care to explain what happened?" I choked out past the laughter trying to obstruct my airway.

The laughter continued as Adam walked towards us grinning. "Ferron got a little amorous with the chocolate fountain and a flamingo."

Ferron groaned, lifting his red face from my chest to twist around and look at Adam. "You bet me, remember?" he accused, sounding mortified. "And I wouldn't have done it if I'd been sober."

I clamped my lower lip between my teeth in an effort to stop the laughter caused by his forlorn expression and the put-upon sigh that followed. "Well, let's take you home and get you cleaned up."

At the tremor in my voice, Ferron's eyes narrowed on me. "Are you laughing at me too, Daddy?" His eyes sparked with humour and... love.

Was it love? Or was I imagining it?

There was no time to think about it further as Nathan asked if I could drop Adam and Richie home. Seeing no way out, I agreed.

Three hours later, I pulled into the drive to find Ferron fast asleep in the seat beside me. Switching off the engine, I turned to stare at him. His dark lashes lay against his pale cheekbones, the scar over his eyebrow barely noticeable now. Even the bruising on his lower jaw was now so faint that I had to look closely in order to spot it.

My heart swelled, cutting off the air in my chest as I recalled Adam and Richie talking about the impromptu party Lenny had thrown. I'd watched Ferron and every time they'd included him in the conversation or talked about something that had happened, his face had glowed with sheer happiness. Happiness that had evoked memories from when he'd first come to the club and found joy in submission.

It was a sobering thought that he'd managed to achieve that without me. Would he eventually leave me and find someone else when he was fully healed? Was I just a stopgap for him? My heart sank as heat gathered at the back of my eye sockets. *Don't go back to hiding! You'll definitely lose him then!*

Yesterday had been the first step in the right direction to claiming back what those fuckers had taken from him. It had to have been a big deal for Ferron, to go from one side of London to the other on his own. Fuck, he'd been so brave. A little stupid, maybe? But brave too.

He'd put himself at risk though and that didn't sit well with me. But he didn't need to know how frantic I'd been while he'd been gone. Not while he was claiming back a little of his independence. He'd done that on his own, and as much as I wanted to smack his bottom for the distress he'd caused that was all that mattered right now.

A wave of weariness swept over me. I got out of the car and unlocked the front door before returning to lift

Ferron out of the passenger seat. Other than burying his face in my neck, he barely stirred. Emotions surfaced at the gesture, my arms tightening around him.

The hair coated in chocolate rubbed against my throat and I chuckled. Drinking from a chocolate fountain while riding a giant stuffed flamingo. Whatever fucking next!

Once inside the house, I locked the door with difficulty, trying not to jostle the sleeping man I held. Carrying him up to the bedroom, I eyed Ferron and then my clean sheets before sighing and walking over to the bed, too tired to do more than lay him down and take off his shoes. After removing my own, I crawled onto the bed next to him. He rolled into me, slinging his arm across my chest with his hand resting against the heart he'd claimed a long time ago. I covered it with mine, sucking in a shaky breath at the softness of his warm skin. The emotional roller coaster I'd ridden the night before seemed to think I needed another ride, making me struggle to catch my breath. The tightness in my chest increased as I dry-heaved. *He's safe. He's safe.*

No matter how many times I repeated it though, the memory of discovering him gone came back to haunt me. As if sensing my distress, Ferron's leg lifted to straddle my thigh, the hand on my chest pressing more firmly against my erratic heart.

Tears slid down my cheeks as I looked up at the ceiling,

What would I have done if they'd taken him?

I would have done anything and everything to get

him back. There was no place on Earth which would have been safe from me if they'd taken away my... heart.

Then talk to him, tell him how you really feel.

Like it's that easy!

Chapter Twelve

Ferron

Feeling nervous, I rubbed my sweaty palms down my jeans as I peeked around the living room door to search for Isaac. He was stood in his favourite position: in front of the big windows which faced the Downs. A place he always seemed to migrate to when he had something on his mind. The darkness outside matched his grim expression and stiff posture. Had I fucked up my chance with him?

My heart trembled in my chest. When I'd woken an hour ago, the space next to me had still been warm from his body so I'd known that Isaac couldn't have got up that long before me. Checking the time had revealed that I'd slept the afternoon away. But being the coward I was,

I'd gone for a shower, changed his sheets and tidied his room. I'd run out of excuses at that point and had had to come downstairs and face the music.

My stomach gurgled so loudly that I cursed under my breath.

Isaac swung around to face me, pinning me in place with a look that I'd hoped never to see on his face: disappointment. As I stepped fully into the room, a ball of panic lodged itself in my throat, my shoulders drooping. Licking my dry lips, I tried to come up with something to say, something that would make up for the frantic messages Isaac had left on my phone.

After Isaac's confession that he'd always liked me, I'd brushed off what that really meant, not wanting to explore my own feelings too closely. Yet as I'd sat on the edge of his bed and plucked up the courage to read the texts, each one more desperate than the last for me to respond, it had torn away the barrier I'd been hiding behind. The only thing was, I didn't know if I was brave enough to show him that even though I was broken, I still wanted to be a part of his life—now and, if he'd have me, forever.

He doesn't want you, nobody does!

"Fuck off!" I gritted out through clenched teeth.

"I beg your pardon," Isaac asked in a strained voice barely recognisable as his, his eyes narrowing on me.

"Nooo! No, not you... I meant the voice in my head. Oh crap... why can't I ever seem to get this right?" I cried out. Tears chilled my cheeks as Isaac scratched his jaw.

"What can't you get right, little man?" Isaac asked in a gentle tone, making no attempt to come closer to me.

The distance between us wasn't working for me, not one little bit. I swiped at my wet cheeks, gazing at him from beneath my eyelashes. There was something about his neutral expression which said I'd be waiting a while for him to make the next move.

Was he waiting for me to take the initiative? Could I do it? *Could I?*

Even as I questioned myself, I hesitated, my eyes imploring Isaac to be the one to make a move. The seconds stretched unbearably between us until I huffed out a defeated breath. "I... Ihavefeelingsforyou," I gushed out all at once, taking a big step towards him at the same time.

I barely stopped myself from rolling my eyes as confusion clouded Isaac's face. Evidently, he couldn't understand my new way of talking: jamming all the words into one big clump. I mean really, how the fuck was I supposed to get through this when my brain and mouth clearly weren't in sync?

Frustration drove me across the floor to stand in front of Isaac, my hands balled at my sides so that I didn't tug at my hair. "I..." *Get on with it, jeez!* This was more painful than watching one of those programs where a woman pushes a tiny human out of her body! "I can do this, I can."

Isaac's brow furrowed. "You can do what?"

Sweet Jesus, save me now. I blew out a breath hard enough to lift my fringe. "I'm sorry I didn't leave you a message to say I was going out. I'm sorry, Daddy, I truly am. And I'm hoping you won't... give up on me now. That... that you still like me even though I was naughty and I upset you." I released a shuddering exhale, but there was no opportunity to congratulate myself for getting all of the words in the right order and for not squishing them together before I was lifted off the floor.

Isaac's dark eyes swirled with such a depth of emotion that it left me mute as I hung suspended in mid-air. "Let's get one thing straight before we talk about how upset I am about last night." His face took on a fierce expression as he paused to lick his lips. "I love you. I've loved you for a long time and nothing, *nothing*, is going to change that. Not even that little stunt you pulled last night."

He loves me. He loves me!

I searched his face for deceit, but all I found was raw emotion.

His chest heaved twice before he gained enough composure to continue. "I was so scared last night when I came home and found you gone. You have no idea how much I tortured myself with what could have happened to you." His eyes shimmered under the lights as he lay his forehead against mine. "Please, dear Gods, never do that to me again," he rasped out, his voice thick with emotion.

"No Daddy, I swear I won't. I wasn't thinking, you see when Lenny called, and if I'm honest, I was a little miffed that you didn't ask me to go with you, I was so excited to be invited out that I forgot about my fear. Well, I did until I got to the train. But Daddy, I did it! I travelled on my own and I didn't freak out. Okay, that might not be completely true, but I didn't make a spectacle of myself so that counts, right?"

When Isaac lifted his head, looking more than a little bewildered, I giggled. "Sorry, I'm talking too fast, aren't I?"

"You are. But it's alright, I got the gist. I think we should order some pizza and then sit and talk through how we both feel about yesterday. Then we'll talk about your punishment for being naughty."

My throat closed over at the word punishment as if it had lodged itself in my airway. All the joy at him saying he loved me fizzled out like a sparkler on Bonfire Night. I wasn't sure what Isaac had read on my face but he gently kissed my lips. "Breathe, little man, breathe. Deep breaths in and out," he whispered against my lips as if offering his own breath to help me.

I followed his instruction until the pain in my chest eased up enough that I could stutter, "pun... ish... ment?"

He carefully lowered me to the floor, cupping my frozen cheeks. "Yes, punishment. But this is not the kind that involves physical or mental torture. I told you when you came into this house that there'd be no punishments of that kind, and I meant it. But what kind of Daddy would I be if I didn't teach my boy that there are consequences for being naughty?" His brows rose and I nodded reluctantly. "Are you okay with waiting until we've sorted out some food?"

Was this part of the punishment?

"Daddy, what if I say no, that I'm not happy to wait?" There was apprehension in my voice which couldn't be avoided. But I was damn happy that I'd managed to say what was on my mind.

"Then we'll talk about it now." His reply was immediate, but I got the feeling that he'd be disappointed in me for not waiting. Would waiting until we'd had food kill me? *Of course not, you fool!*

I sighed. "I'll wait until we've had food, Daddy." I'd barely finished speaking before Isaac was beaming at me, pride shining in his eyes.

Unfortunately, that smile didn't help me to get through the hour that followed, an hour which felt like the longest of my life. My nerves were stretched to the point that I felt like I might vomit if I ate.

Isaac, on the other hand, dug right in. After he'd practically inhaled two slices of pizza, he eyed me over the third slice. "You're not hungry?"

"I don't think I could swallow it, Daddy," I mumbled, dropping my gaze to the table while my fingers traced a pattern on the wood. "Can you tell me now what my... punishment is going to be?" I held my breath as he finished off the third slice, his face an unreadable mask.

He licked his fingers before taking a drink of water from the glass sat in front of him. I thought I was going to explode by the time he finally answered me.

"There are two parts to the punishment." He gave a wicked smile and my heart took flight. "So, the first part of your penance is that I get to pick where we go on our first date. There will be no whining about my choice of restaurant or"—the wicked smile turned wolfish —"movie. The second part we'll discuss after our date."

I breathed out a dreamy sigh. *He wants to take me on a date. Well, I never!*

What about the second part of the punishment?

Oh, stop spoiling it!

Chapter Thirteen

Isaac

"Calm the fuck down, Isaac, seriously. I only got half of what you said between all the cussing you were doing," Nathan growled, his face pinched as he rubbed his temple.

Exhaling gustily, I plonked myself down in the chair in front of his desk, making it creak loudly. I checked my watch knowing that I didn't have a great deal of time before Nix would arrive, or I needed to go back down to the bar.

After Nix had sent me a cryptic text saying he wanted to meet me as soon as possible, it had been hard enough to leave Ferron downstairs. I'd arranged for him to come to the club so Ferron wouldn't be suspicious. I hadn't yet plucked up the courage to tell him that I'd hired security men to watch over him when I wasn't around. I rubbed at my jaw as I stared at Nathan's fathomless expression. "Sorry, I'm just—"

Nathan interrupted before I got a chance to finish. "Pissed off, frustrated, angry, annoyed—"

"Okay, you don't need to go on. What I was trying to do was explain why I've got a friend coming here. I don't want to upset Ferron with whatever Nix has discovered about the shit Devon's involved in. I need privacy to talk to him and I thought it was best to bring you in on this because I've got a feeling it will delay the court case."

"Are you kidding me?" Nathan stood up so fast that his seat shot back. He didn't notice though as he came around the desk and stood over me, anger sparking in his eyes.

I held my hands up to ward him off. "I know Lenny is as stressed as Ferron about this and I'm sorry, I really am. But what if there are more men out there, men who are trapped the same way Ferron was?" I ground out through clenched teeth.

After mulling over what Ferron had told me, I'd confided in Nathan knowing that at some point it was all going to come out publicly. The court case was looming and as much as I wanted this over for Ferron's sake. I couldn't, in all good conscience, let go of the possibility that there were others out there suffering too.

Before I got a chance to say more, a knock came on Nathan's office door, Gabriel's head appearing through the gap. Gabriel's face lit up with a killer smile that usually had all the subs in the club chasing him which usually amused the hell out of me. Today though, all I felt was frustration and the urge to tell him to get lost. When Nix appeared behind him, my brow furrowed. I had no time to question what was going on as Phil Knight stepped around both men. The small office was now full of alpha males, my gaze moving between all three men. "What the fuck is this?"

My heart rate knew damn well what this was though as I recalled the fact that Gabriel did freelance security work. *Fuck, had he been following Ferron?*

Knowing Gabriel's reputation, my eyes narrowed on him.

"Isaac, you're giving me the creeps. Why are you looking at me like that?" he asked pleasantly enough, but something shifting in his eyes said differently. He stepped farther into the room without having been invited, his posture changing to something that resembled a battle stance.

"Have you been following Ferron?" I asked without any preamble.

If I hadn't been watching him closely, I might have missed his lips pinch for a second.

"Why? You worried, big man?" His large frame relaxed as he leaned against the wall, both Nix and Phil giving off an air of casualness that I knew was fake.

"If you two are going to have a pissing match, can you do it later as I've got a shitload on my plate at the moment?" Phil interjected, his brow arching as he took the seat opposite, Nathan moving back around his desk to sit.

The air thickened with tension and I scratched my unshaven jaw. "Why are you here, Phil?"

"Shit, didn't I mention that it's Phil's security firm that

I work for?" Nix said. His shoulders lifted to shrug off my accusatory glare.

He knew fucking full well that he hadn't mentioned who his boss was. Nathan's chair creaked and I glanced over at him. His face was full of concern, but he remained silent as I shifted my gaze to the other men in the room.

Nix's expression turned thoughtful as he rubbed at the back of his neck. "Security Specialist Advisors, SSA, for short. I mentioned the name to you and it will be on the paperwork you filled in and signed."

"Yeah, okay." I glanced at Phil. "I wasn't aware it was your company."

"You got a problem with me?" Phil's face was unreadable, but his voice was tight.

"Nope, but I like to know who I have working for me. Why didn't you mention the name of your security firm before? Like when you helped to ramp up security at New Year?" I glanced over at Nathan as he coughed, my brows drawing together. "Is there something else going on here?"

"No, well, nothing apart from trying to work out who is sabotaging the progress of the Flamingo Bar, which I've already discussed with you," Nathan replied, sounding more than a little pissed off.

"We seem to have gotten off track. Shall we get back to why we're here?" asked Phil, his question seemingly directed at me.

"The floor is yours," I offered, the skin at the nape of my neck tingling.

I shifted my attention to Gabriel as he sighed. The killer smile was long gone, replaced by a thin-lipped grimace. His hand ruffled his hair as it raked through it, his expression showing a resignation which twisted my insides painfully. "Several months ago, SSA were hired by a wealthy family to look for their estranged son. They'd had a falling out when they found out he was gay, but before they got a chance to make up he'd disappeared. Months of searching led me to the Dom's Haven."

His face became an impenetrable mask. "What I found, well, let's just say that in comparison this place would be a beauty spa, and that would be a dog fighting pit. You were right to be worried about the possibility of there being other men out there caught up in the same web of deceit as Ferron. They seem to ferret out men with no family to check up on them, like Ferron. Then they pick a Dom for them. After that, it becomes a little less clear what happens because the Doms there are a lot less talkative to other Doms that haven't been part of the club for that long."

Gabriel released a frustrated sigh. His eyes were full of fire though. "I don't have any bloody trouble imagining what Devon did to Ferron, but finding someone else to talk about it, now that's the fucking sticking point."

Trapped and being forced to do...

I left the thought unfinished because I didn't want to chase the Mad Hatter into a crazy world, not in front of these men. And my vivid imagination didn't need any more fuel, but that didn't help with the feeling in my gut which said that Ferron might have been luckier than some of the others.

Phil spoke next, a chill running through me at his words. "After Nix filled me in on all the background info about Ferron, I started to put two and two together. I don't think it's a coincidence that it was the same club that we're investigating over the other young man's disappearance. Do you think Ferron would be willing to talk frankly about what happened?"

I swallowed the urge to say no, shrugging as I reminded myself that it wasn't my decision. "He's seeing a psychologist and he is starting to talk about it... but it's... it's hard for him." I left it at that, not wanting to go into just how difficult it was for him. They didn't need to know that he'd acted like a wounded animal after opening up to me. No, that was my own private hell, one I'd never forget.

"Is he working today?" Gabriel asked, interrupting my thoughts.

"He is." I checked my watch, cursing as I got up out of the seat. "He's downstairs and probably wondering where I've got to."

Gabriel's face lit up.

I held my hands up. "We're not rushing this. Ferron has to take the lead on this, not you, not any of you. Got it?" The grim expressions on all the men's faces twisted my insides, but I stood firm. I couldn't find it in me to give a shit about them. Ferron was my priority and I'd make damn sure that everyone else knew that. "I gotta go. I'll speak to him and if he's happy to talk to you, Phil, then I'll let you know."

"When?" asked Phil, before I'd even taken a step towards the door.

I swallowed a sigh, understanding why he was so impatient but not liking it one little bit. "Gimme ten minutes and I'll call up from the bar if he's happy to talk." With my nerves stretched to breaking point, I left, taking the stairs two at a time. I needed Ferron, needed to hold him, to feel him pressed against me.

Breathless and sweaty as I entered the bar, Ferron turned in my direction. A smile spread slowly across his face, my heart thudding painfully against my ribs at the knowledge of what I was about to do.

Chapter Fourteen

Ferron

After checking my phone for the umpteenth time, I shoved it into the back pocket of my jeans. What was keeping Isaac?

It was at his insistence that I kept my phone on me at all times, even when he was with me. And okay, the fact that he wanted to be able to speak to me all the time did make me feel all gooey inside. But I'd become a little obsessed with checking it frequently, concerned that I might not have heard it ring or felt it vibrate.

Ever since Adam's stag party, Isaac had stayed within a few feet of me. His gaze never wandered from me for too long, not that I was complaining. Being the centre of his attention was intoxicating, but it could still be a little overwhelming at times. He never bothered to hide the love shining from his eyes and, boy, oh boy, did it make it hard at times to resist rubbing myself all over him. I wanted all the subs in the club to know that he belonged to me. Yet I held back, holding his declaration of love to me like a mother would her newborn baby to her chest. The wonderment of it stayed with me, making it hard not to say the words back to him.

Was it love I felt for him? Or was I confusing it with gratitude?

I'd talked it over with Mark at my last appointment, pondering aloud why I couldn't say the words back to Isaac. He'd suggested writing down the feelings that came to mind whenever I thought about Isaac. On the surface it had seemed like a good idea. But after filling two A4 sides of paper in four hours, I'd realised that I thought about him a lot.

The new bedtime routine Isaac had initiated made it almost impossible for there to be anything other than him in my head though. I gave a heartfelt sigh, fanning my face as a wave of heat rode up my neck and into my cheeks.

The new routine had come about after the discussion about punishment. I wasn't sure whether it was the second part that he'd alluded to but never elaborated on. It certainly felt like it though, given the sexual torment Isaac was making me endure. Alright, maybe endure wasn't the right word. But after he'd bathed me thoroughly, got me ready for bed and then finally tucked me in with kisses that left me hard and aching, it was a close call.

If that wasn't bad enough, he'd started to give me rules. Some were definitely easier than others, like having the phone. But the one about not touching myself was a whole different ball game. The sub in me wanted to please him, whereas the boy who liked to be a little bratty wanted to touch.

With the memory of how much I'd wanted to beg him not to leave me alone in bed the previous night still fresh in my mind, I looked around the room searching for a distraction. A smile spread across my face at the sight of how I'd made the glass, polished metal and wood on the bar gleam. After Isaac had gone to speak to Nathan, I'd used the time alone to finish setting up the bar for tonight. I wiggled and danced on the spot. Date night. It was date night.

It had felt like the longest few days in the history of all the days since Isaac had said we were going to have a night out. He'd struggled to jiggle the staff around to make it happen sooner, one of the stand-in bar managers going off sick and the other having some sort of family crisis and unable to swap with Isaac. So I'd impatiently waited for today to arrive and I couldn't wait to see where Isaac was going to take me.

I eyed my smart jeans and the fitted pink Henley shirt I'd splurged on, hoping that I'd picked the right outfit for the night. I chewed on my lip, catching my expression in the mirror. I clapped my hands and gave a little squeal of delight at my sparkling eyes and unmarked face, looking around to check that no one had snuck up on me. *Look at me! I'm... happy.*

A tear slid down my cheek and I swiped at it, letting the emotions settle in my chest right next to the warmth of Isaac's love. The two were a perfect compliment. I froze for a second, my eyes widening. *I love him. I love Isaac!*

You're unlovable!

"I'm not!" I stamped my foot as if I could grind the negative thoughts into the ground. I clung on to the memory of Isaac declaring his love for me, thinking about how his eyes had glowed with a fierce passion. "I'm loveable! I am." I spoke with as much conviction as I could muster.

With love back in the driving seat, I danced back to the bar, humming with excitement at the thought of sharing my revelation with Isaac. Maybe I could do it when he took me for the meal?

As the door that led upstairs opened, a grin spread across my face. It faltered though as I caught sight of Isaac's worried expression. Needing to remove the concern from his face, I walked silently across the wooden floor. I stopped in front of him, my heart sinking when his lips appeared to tremble before he firmed them. "What happened?"

"I have a question to ask, but know that you can say no if you want to." Isaac's chest moved rapidly, his hands balling at his sides as I gave a tentative nod.

"I'm not sure whether you've ever met Phil Knight? He's the security guy Nathan employed after ...after Devon's attack on you. Anyway, he's upstairs and he'd like to talk to you about your experience at the Dom's Haven."

Isaac's voice sounded as if his vocal cords had been rubbed with sandpaper. He spoke calmly, but I didn't miss the way the muscles in his jaw twitched to reveal that he wasn't as calm as he made out. That fact alone stopped me from turning tail and running. The desire to hide from something I wasn't ready to relive was strong.

There was something in the depths of Isaac's gaze though that made me swallow the instinctive refusal. "Okay, Daddy. You won't leave me alone though, will you?" My chin trembled and my legs almost buckled at his headshake.

"Never, little man. I'll be with you all the time if that's what you want?"

"I do, Daddy," I choked out past the panic wanting to take hold of me. I whimpered as Isaac swept me up into his arms. "Daddy I'm scared. What if... what if you don't—"

His lips pressed gently to mine stopping me from uttering another word. The tender kiss was so sweet that I sighed and melted into his arms. He kept it gentle, his lips exploring mine until I opened up and his tongue slid over mine. I groaned in delight as his taste flooded my mouth.

"There is nothing you could say that will change my feelings. I. Love. You." He punctuated each word with a soft kiss.

Seeing my eye roll as he moved away, Isaac chuckled. "Don't forget that Daddy will punish you for being cheeky." His threat lost any credibility as I spotted the humour dancing in his eyes.

I wasn't stupid though; I still had an unknown punishment coming up. So I quickly apologised. He lowered me back to the ground and I was reminded of the reason he'd kissed me in the first place. My hands clasped together. Could I do this?

"Are you sure you want to do this?" asked Isaac, as if he'd somehow read my mind.

"Yes, yes I... want to." Given the way my heart was slamming against my ribs that might have been a slight exaggeration. I clamped my lips together as Isaac took his phone out of his pocket and searched for a number.

It's all going to be fine. Isaac will stay with me.

I couldn't drown out the utter lack of conviction in the voice inside my head.

At least it's my voice and not...

Nope, not going there!

Chapter Fifteen

Isaac

All the big plans I'd had for tonight seemed frivolous and stupid after hearing what Ferron had suffered at Devon's hands. At the hands of a circle of men who were nothing more than human traffickers. Only those fuckers pedalled in subs who were alone in the world.

Fucking shitty bastards!

After Phil had left Nathan's office with the information he'd wanted, Ferron had crawled into my lap and wept inconsolably in my arms. Any thoughts of not being able to cope with whatever Ferron revealed were obliterated. He had torn a big hole right in the centre of my chest and eviscerated my heart.

He'd been fucking raped, beaten—tortured!

How did someone get over that and move on with

their life? A shudder rippled through me. It made Ferron's reaction to getting an erection all the more understandable now that I had the full back story. I cringed at the thought of the bedtime regime I'd initiated. I'd been hoping to make Ferron feel more comfortable about being naked and aroused. But now I felt like a sleazy bastard and was worried I'd made things worse for him.

He gets aroused. That means you're doing something right, doesn't it?

Shaking off the thought that I'd made a huge misstep with Ferron, I closed my eyes and exhaled a shuddery breath.

After seeing his red swollen eyes and sorrowful expression, I'd brought him home at a loss to how else I could comfort him. When we'd got there, he'd gone straight upstairs without saying anything so I'd let him be. That had been thirty minutes ago and I'd come to stare out of the window, feeling like shit that I couldn't take away what had happened to him.

Would killing Devon be worth prison time?

My hands clenched at my sides at the thought of choking the bastard to death. I tilted my head at the sound of floorboards creaking, swinging around as Ferron walked into the room a short while later. His face was pale and his eyes were a little puffy but they were no longer red-rimmed. The biggest difference though was the light in his gaze. It had been full of defeat when he'd left me, but now... well, I wasn't sure what had replaced it. What I did know was that it made my belly dance with nerves as his gaze swept over me from head to toe. "I—"

"Daddy, are you wearing your work clothes to go out tonight?" Ferron asked, pouting as he gave me another inspection.

I had to swallow twice before I could speak. "I wasn't sure you'd want to go out after..." Taking the cowards way out I left the sentence hanging, not wanting to re-hash what he'd spoken about earlier. No, there'd be plenty of time for that over the coming months.

"He's taken enough from me. He's not stealing my first date with you as well. He's not!" He stamped his foot on the floor, his hands moving to his waist as his chin jutted out.

Pride at his bravery swelled inside me. If he could be brave, then I needed to show him that I could be too. I stood up straighter. "I'll be ten minutes."

"You better not make us late, Daddy."

I coughed, doing my best to disguise a chuckle. Fuck, he was adorable. He looked about as fierce as a baby rabbit, but I kept that thought to myself. I flicked my finger down his nose as I passed. "I promise I won't make us late."

I didn't hear one word that Adam said as he led us through the restaurant. Chancing a quick look at Ferron's face, my stomach dropped. It was an unreadable mask as he glanced around the gorgeous restaurant. The dreamy pink lighting cast a lovely glow over the tables. Glassware and cutlery sparkled on the tables as we passed. The soft romantic music playing in the background was perfectly pitched to allow muted conversations between diners. Not that I was worried about that as I'd paid an additional fee to hire the private dining room wanting this night to be special.

I'd pulled every string I could to get the place at such short notice. The restaurant was usually booked up months in advance, but I'd convinced Carl to talk Seb into giving me the private room for tonight. Carl had bitched about it, but with his wedding coming up at the weekend there'd been very little heat in his rant about me taking advantage of our friendship.

As we reached the door that led into the private room, I started to have second thoughts about my over-the-top gesture. Ferron had been a nervous wreck in the car plucking constantly at the seat belt, his leg tapping out of time with the music on the radio. Once I'd pulled into the car park at the side of La Trattoria Di Amore's main restaurant, his eyes had widened to the point where his face was almost consumed by them.

I tuned back in to what Adam was saying as he pulled the door open. "Here we are. I've made sure that everything's in place, Isaac." Adam gave me a sly wink as he stepped out of the way to reveal the room to Ferron.

Ferron's sharp inhale was followed by a choked sob. His eyes gleamed with unshed tears as he looked from the open doorway to me. "You... you did this for me?" A solitary tear slid down his cheek, his chin trembling.

Oh Christ, don't cry. Don't cry! I silently pleaded.

The table in the centre of the room was set for two people. The crisp white tablecloth complimented the deep pink Stargazer Orchids I'd sourced and had delivered. Their subtle scent was still discernible over the heavenly aroma of food coming through the door from the main restaurant.

The table setting was the same as in the main dining room, with the exception of the silver ice bucket at the side of the table. It held a bottle of Veuve Clicquot champagne. One that had been recommended after I'd explained Ferron's preference for a sweeter wine.

Adam patted my arm reassuringly. I gave him a curt nod and he left discreetly, but not before I'd noticed his amusement. I'd pre-ordered the meal with all of Ferron's favourites so Adam wasn't needed. I struggled to gauge whether I'd done the right thing as I ushered Ferron into the room, not wanting to give the other patrons a show if he hated it.

Ferron swung around as the door shut, puckering his mouth for a kiss. I swept him into my arms and held him for a second, looking into his teary eyes. Emotions flickered across his face so fast that I didn't even attempt to decipher them. I slowly lowered my mouth to his, pressing my lips gently against him. His breathy sigh caused my groin to flood with heat.

His hands crept around my neck, his fingers weaving into the hair at my nape and tugging me closer to him. I groaned as his lower body pressed firmly against me. The heat of his arousal felt like it was branding me. My arms tightened around him as his mouth opened and his tongue boldly swept over my lips.

All the blood in my head moved south as I strained to keep control. Days of touching him without following through with all of the things I'd wanted to do melded into a hot ball of lust as his hips rocked against me in wanton abandon.

Keep control, keep control. You're a Dom for fuck's sake!

Explain that to my other head because right now it doesn't want to listen.

The internal debate was sufficient for me to regain a slight modicum of control. I gasped. "We need to stop or you'll never get the meal I've planned for you."

IIis mouth glistened in the light as he licked his lips. My groin tightened painfully as I imagined what that tongue could do to me.

Tortured, raped... get a fucking grip!

The thought was similar to the icy bucket of water poured over me during the ice bucket challenge a few years back. It had the same effect as well and I shuddered. Ferron's brow knitted together so I quickly reassured him. "Sit and let me pamper you." Giving him the biggest smile I could, I tugged on his hand. "I hope you like the menu I've planned for tonight."

He let me seat him at the table. I opened the champagne and poured a glass for him to taste. "Try it, I'm hoping it's sweet enough?" I felt heat move up my neck as his head tilted to one side before he picked up the champagne flute.

The air seemed to disappear as he sipped the wine,

letting it linger in his mouth. His eyelashes fluttered as he moaned in delight.

"This is yummy, and you can sure as heck taste the difference from a bottle of Asti, that's for sure." He sounded breathless as he spoke. His eyes revealed a wealth of feelings that I struggled to interpret. *Did he feel the same about me as I did about him?*

The door opened to reveal Adam and a waiter holding two plates. By the time the starter had been explained, Ferron's full focus was on the plate in front of him, my question going unanswered.

Coward.

Chapter Sixteen

Ferron

After a beautiful meal and watching the movie *Dolittle*
I'd mentioned wanting to see, the urge to pinch myself to
check that this wasn't a dream was strong. But then after
Isaac had helped me off with my coat and escorted me
into the living room, he dropped a bombshell.

My lips flapped open, the bubbles from the champagne feeling like they'd become lodged in my brain and
made me start hearing things. I stared at Isaac across the
living room. "You want me to do what?" I shrieked.
When he chuckled at my alarm, I wished for the floor to
open up and swallow me

"You heard me, little man. I want you to tie me to the
bed and then explore my body. As I already explained,

this is the second part of your punishment." His dark brows arched but he looked relaxed.

The deep timbre of his voice was like a sexy caress and I balled my hands to stop them from wandering towards the cock firmly pressed against my fly. From the moment he'd mentioned getting naked and letting me have free rein over his body, I'd got so hard that I was sure my cock was going to rip right through the fabric of my jeans.

Could I do it, could I touch him and not freak out? The last time a man had been naked in front of me he'd... *You can stop that right now. This is Isaac, he'd never hurt you—ever.*

"I... you see... how... why?" I screwed my eyes tightly shut and stamped my foot. *Spit it out!*

I jerked at the feel of Isaac's warm hands cupping my face, my eyes instantly opening. "Devon took away your control. I want to give it back to you in the only way I know how. I want you to feel confident that you're in charge. And that nothing will happen without your say so."

His eyes crinkled as he offered me a smile that took my breath away, allaying a little of the fear that was mixed in with the excitement at what he was offering me. "But you're a Dom."

"That may be so, but am I not your Daddy too? Does a Daddy not take care of all of his boy's needs?" His eyes darkened with desire, and with love, holding me captive.

"Yes, yes, Daddy, but what if—"

"There are no what ifs. There's just you and me and

exploring your boundaries." Isaac's fingers gently caressed my face. "Are you going to take your punishment like a good boy?" His eyes sparkled with humour.

It wasn't lost on me that this could be just as much of a punishment for him as it was for me. He let go of my face before offering me one of his hands to hold. I exhaled shakily, knowing what he was silently asking. This was my decision regardless of how he'd wrapped it up. My fingers were trembling as I took his outstretched hand, linking our fingers together. "Yes, Daddy."

His chest heaved as he led me up to his bedroom. I stood and watched as he walked around the massive bed, attaching several long pieces of silk to the bedposts. He tugged on them to show that they were secure before glancing in my direction, a wicked smile forming on his lips.

The smile briefly disappeared as he tugged his black cashmere jumper over his head and dropped it on the floor. His white shirt went next, by which point I was struggling not to swallow my tongue. His massive hairy chest was a thing of beauty that made me want to curl up on it and snuggle.

That idea had disappeared by the time his shoes, socks and trousers were in a pile on the floor. Only navy boxer briefs were left which looked as if they were struggling to contain the cock inside them. If I'd been in any doubt that Isaac found the idea of being tied up appealing, his cock showed how far from the truth that was. A dark wet patch spreading across the fabric revealed his excitement, my gaze lingering on his groin.

"You like what you see, little man?" he rasped in a husky voice.

I tried to swallow, but coughed when my tight throat wouldn't obey. I nodded instead.

"I'm going to leave my boxers on. Unless you want me to take them off?"

"Off," I croaked out, my mouth running away with itself before my brain could catch up. Heat spread across my face but I kept my gaze fixed on Isaac. His eyes lit up with approval as he pushed down his underwear, his cock slapping against his abdomen. *Holy fuck, he's huge!*

My thighs squeezed together and my pucker clenched. Isaac's large hand stroked his cock from base to tip in one fluid move. The lamps he'd lit at either side of the bed illuminated him in a soft light. His large body was covered in dark hair, my gaze moving back to his cock with curiosity. The hair at the base of his erection was trimmed but it was still thick, like a pelt of fur. For the first time in... forever, I wanted to touch someone.

My hands trembled with, what I was coming to understand as need, need for this man. "Can I touch, Daddy?" My voice was barely a whisper but Isaac still heard me, nodding and swallowing hard enough to make his Adam's apple bob furiously.

In the time it took to close the four steps which separated us, a bead of pre-cum was sitting on the tip of Isaac's cock. His hard length was dusky pink, the vein running up the side looking as if it was pulsing in time to his heartbeat. I glanced at him from beneath my eyelashes as I tentatively reached out to touch the tip.

He hissed as my finger slid across the slick tip gently rubbing the pre-cum over the head. His hands balled at his sides, but his body remained still. Although, my focus was solely on the head of his cock which seemed to swell more with each caress of my fingertip. The scent of his cum was heady and my mouth watered for a taste.

Would he ram it into my throat and try and suffocate me?

No, no he won't. He's given you control, take it.

The thought wouldn't let go though as I weighed up whether I had enough courage to tie Isaac to the bed.

"Little man... give me a second," Isaac said through gritted teeth.

It was only then that I realised I was still stroking the slick head of his cock. The floor had several dark marks on it between his naked feet. His jaw clenched as he slowly took a step towards the bed. He was flushed and his face was sheened with sweat. Had he been about to come?

His painfully hard cock bobbed drawing my gaze. His low-hanging balls were tight to his body and his thighs were quivering. My eyes widened as I stared at Isaac in wonderment. He'd been going to come just from my finger touching his cock? *Jeez Louise!*

A smile tugged at my cheeks as I saw him register what had been about to happen. "Daddy, were you about to come?" I asked in breathy astonishment.

"Yes, for fuck's sake!" he growled.

"Oh Daddy, you're naughty. You put me in charge, right?" At his reluctant nod, my smile grew. "That means you can't come unless I say so. You better get on the bed so I can tie you up."

I giggled at the expletives he muttered under his breath. But he did as I'd asked lying spread-eagled on the bed. I rubbed my hands together and eyed him. "Where to start?" I tapped at my lips.

He shook his head. "I've created a monster." He sighed mournfully but his cock continued to leak over his stomach.

"Daddy, I'm just taking my punishment like a good boy," I said, chuckling. I walked over to the foot of the bed and tied the silk bindings to his ankles before moving to do the same to his arms. His muscles flexed and bulged as he settled on the patterned duvet beneath him. I crawled onto the bed at his left side and gently stroked his chest. The hair was silky soft against my palm. He murmured encouragement and pushed into my hand. A heady feeling of exhilaration poured through my veins as I used my other hand to stroke his thigh, tracing the muscle definition. His cock bobbed and dripped, a pool of pearly liquid gathering on his lower belly.

I licked my lips as I met Isaac's heavy-lidded gaze. His whole body quivered as I slowly lowered my mouth to taste.

Chapter Seventeen

Isaac

The ache in my jaw turned into a throbbing pain as I gritted my teeth straining to keep still beneath the torment of Ferron's soft strokes. It was as if he planned to slowly drive me mad with each gentle caress. Over the years, I'd been in some extreme situations but none had brought me to my knees in quite the same way as Ferron was doing. I was grateful to be lying down, convinced that I would have embarrassed myself and fallen to the floor if not.

Fuck, my whole body felt weak from his tentative touches. They were brutally arousing to the point where I was convinced I could come without him even having touched my cock. As if he'd sensed I was close to losing it, his gaze met mine, my chest tightening. The desire in his eyes slayed me, my cock bucking as his gaze moved to my stomach, his intention becoming clear.

Holy motherfucker!

The air refused to leave my lungs as the tip of his tongue lapped at the pre-cum pooling on my stomach. He whimpered, his hands stilling on my body and his mouth opening wider as if he couldn't get enough. The flat of his tongue dragged over my flesh sending ripples of pleasure straight to my cock, which bobbed close to his cheek as if it was trying to draw his attention.

"Fuckkkkk," I ground out. My arms strained against the bindings, a full body shudder pressing Ferron's clothed body against mine. The feel of his tongue lapping at the slit of my cock was exquisite, his tongue circling the head of my cock as his eyelids lowered to shield his expression. I knew he was enjoying himself though from the slurping noises and the way his fingers clenched and unclenched.

When I'd thought of giving up control to Ferron, whatever my expectations had been, it hadn't been this painful arousal. My focus had been on him finding ways to claim back the freedom that had been stolen from him. Hell, I'd even spoken to Mark about handing control over to Ferron. The fucker had encouraged me.

A groan rumbled through my chest and I gasped as Ferron cupped my heavy balls in his hand. His mouth continued to tease the mushroom head of my cock. With both Ferron's mouth and hand tormenting me, I wanted to beg for mercy and kick my own arse for thinking I could cope with this. *Cope! That was a fucking joke!* I wanted to cry like a baby and plead to be able to come.

Then his lips encircled the head of my cock and his cheeks hollowed. The cry that left me would have been embarrassing if I hadn't already been garbling. "Please let me come, oh fuck pleaseeee."

"Daddy, has no one taught you that you need to be patient?" Ferron asked in a husky tone that caused shivers to skitter down my spine and lodge in my arse.

His hot breath teased my cock as he gazed up at me. His eyes sparkled with confidence, desire and humour. The look alone would have been hard enough to resist, but when the tip of his tongue licked at his lips in a provocative manner I was done for.

A loud buzzing started up in my ears, sweat gathering on my skin as I strained to get closer to his lips. "Little man, Daddy needs you."

The second the words left my mouth he returned his lips to my cock. Warm, wet heat encased the head as he swirled his tongue across the tip of my cock before dipping into my slit. At the same time, he gently squeezed my balls, air exploding out of my chest. I lurched up as far as the bindings would allow, flinging my head back. "Holyyyyyyy shittttttt!"

Every muscle in my body twitched, sensations overwhelming me to the point where black spots appeared in front of my eyes. Endless spurts of cum shot painfully out of my cock. Ferron whimpered, moaned and wriggled at my side, not releasing me until he'd drunk me dry.

There was such smug satisfaction on his face as he shifted back on his heels that my lips moved into a lazy grin as I collapsed back on the damp cover. "Feeling pretty happy with yourself, aren't you?" I rasped out breathlessly.

His brows arched. "Who me, Daddy?" Then he spoilt it by giggling, his eyes alight with a mischievous smile.

"Yes, you," I chuckled, too exhausted to say anything more.

"You came like a freight train."

Even though I was knackered, the way he was eyeing my spent cock made the fucking thing twitch as if it was preparing for round two. As I shifted, my arms gave a twinge and I groaned, but not in pleasure. "Can you untie Daddy now?"

Ferron's forehead gained several deep lines as he glanced at his lap. He climbed off the bed, his hands balling at his sides.

What's this about?

Without saying a word he untied my ankles, gently rubbing at the red marks marring my skin. My feet tingled as the blood flow returned fully. I resigned myself to the same thing happening with my arms as I tried to relax them.

It was only when Ferron seemed to hesitate, dragging his feet as he moved to the head of the bed that I focused my attention back on him. My stomach fluttered. Trying not to second guess myself over what had just happened, I asked gently, "Is everything alright, little man?"

He stood rooted to the spot, his lower lip disappearing between his teeth. He lowered his head to hide his expression, his rigid posture sending my pulse skyrocketing.

"You won't be cross with me, will you?"

"Cross about what, little man?" Panic gripped my heart and twisted it at how defeated he sounded. It didn't abate as he continued to stare at the ground. "Talk to me, little man."

His eyelashes fluttered as his gaze met mine. Tears glistened in his eyes. "Daddy, I came in my pants," he whispered, his expression full of despair.

I swallowed past the hard knot which had formed in my throat and gave him a tremulous smile. "Come and untie, Daddy. I need a hug."

Thankfully, his tears didn't fall as he moved with hesitation to undo the bindings. The rush of blood proved as painful as I'd suspected it would, but the need to show Ferron he'd done nothing wrong took precedence over my own discomfort.

I kept my moves slow and easy. Taking hold of his hand, I encouraged him onto the bed next to me. I lifted him to lie against me tucking his head under my chin. He lifted his hand and lay it over my heart. My sinuses burned as I blinked, hoping the ache at the back of my eyes would subside. Love surged through me as I rocked him kissing the top of his head several times.

He sniffed and rubbed his cheek against the hair on my chest.

Only when his body had melted against mine, did I speak. "Can you tell me why you're upset about coming?"

He stiffened, but then went lax as I did nothing more than stroke his back.

Had I made it a rule he couldn't come? I didn't think I had. I had put in a rule about him not touching his cock though. Did he think that meant no coming?

"I was never allowed to come, not without permission. He never gave me permission, not that I needed it anyway because I hated what he did to me and I never got hard. He just didn't notice. But with you, Daddy, I was so hard. Then you came and I couldn't hold back until it was too late. I'm sorry, Daddy... you won't punish me... will you?"

It was all said in one big, breathless rush, each word ploughing into my guts more effectively than a punch. The tears burning my eyes slid down my hot cheeks. My jaw clenched as I worked to keep my hold gentle, all the while struggling to swallow. Needing him to look at me, I tucked a finger beneath his chin, lifting it so that he could see the distress on my face over what he'd suffered. His lips quivered as his gaze met mine.

"I'm so sorry, little man. Daddy should have been more specific with you so that you didn't get upset. You. Have. Done. Nothing. Wrong." I punctuated each word with a kiss to the tip of his nose. "This is Daddy's fault for not talking about the rules properly. What do you think about making a joint list of rules for the pair of us?"

His eyes lit up, the despair disappearing. "You mean I get to write some for you?" He wriggled against me. The fabric of his jeans rubbed my sensitive cock and I had to bite back a moan.

"Yes, absolutely. You can write down the rules for Daddy and I'll write yours. Then we can see if we're happy with them and put them up on the wall in the kitchen."

He nodded eagerly. "I'd like that." He gave me a beaming smile and a quick kiss before all but jumping off me.

"What are you doing?"

He rolled his eyes at me. "I'm going to get some pens and paper, silly."

My lips twitched at the bratty response as he sailed out of the room. I'd created a bloody monster. I huffed out a breath and covered my eyes.

A monster you love with everything inside you!

That was the bloody truth, and I couldn't find a thing wrong with it.

Chapter Eighteen

Ferron

The street was busy as I exited the taxi on the opposite side of the road to where I needed to be. Roadworks had stopped the cabbie from being able to drop me outside Mark's building. Isaac had had too much to do today at work to take me to my appointment so he'd organised a taxi. It was a thoughtful gesture somehow ruined by how blasé he'd been about me going on my own.

Had sleeping in my own bed after our date night messed things up?

After locating paper and pens, I'd returned to Isaac's bedroom only to find him snoring softly. Watching him in that unguarded moment, my heart had swelled with the love I'd been refusing to believe was real. Those feelings wouldn't be denied though, not after what we'd just experienced together. It had been the most profound moment of my life, my body taking over as I stopped worrying what would happen to me. I'd all but entered subspace when Isaac had come in my mouth. His total loss of control had acted as an aphrodisiac, my cock revelling in the moment.

Isaac's heavy-lidded, satisfied expression had made me get lost in him, lost in the pleasure I'd given him. But then my sticky pants had shoved the reality in my face of what I'd done without permission. With the fear back in charge, he'd shown me why my heart knew better than my head, shown me why I loved him. Any hopes I'd had of protecting my heart from him had disappeared at his reaction. That night had changed something that I'd thought was damaged beyond repair. The gentleness of his touch and the way he'd shouldered the blame had wiped away my defences like nothing else could. They'd fallen faster than a row of dominoes.

Yet, as I'd stood at the bottom of the bed clutching the paper and pens, I hadn't been able to make myself climb into the bed with him. Oh, I'd wanted to more than anything, but my old rejection insecurities had stopped me cold. So instead of doing as I'd wanted, I'd left him sleeping and showered before crawling into my lonely bed.

The following morning, Isaac hadn't mentioned anything about it when he'd awoken, which had made it harder to broach the subject of sleeping permanently in his bed. It had been all I'd been able to think about for the last few days, and what I needed to talk to Mark about today.

I was confused by Isaac's behaviour and concerned that after what I'd confessed to Phil that maybe Isaac didn't want me anymore.

Oh, give over, he said he loves you.

Then why hasn't he asked me to sleep in his bed?

Ask him for Pete's sake!

Distracted, I rubbed my neck as people hurried past me paying me no attention. A creepy sensation slithered down my spine and I eyed the faces of those around me as I walked over to the pedestrian crossing. The traffic noise seemed to disappear as my ears buzzed. *You're okay, no one is going to hurt you. Isaac promised.*

The thought helped a little as I worked to slow my breathing. As memories of what had happened before started to surface, I exhaled gustily, all but running across the road as the green light started to flash.

By the time I'd got to the curb on the other side, sweat had gathered on my brow even with the chilly February wind. I snuggled into my coat, hurrying towards the glass-fronted building where Mark's office was. The sensation of being watched increased as I pushed the door open and stepped into the warm foyer. Acting as casually as I could, I glanced back at the street. I couldn't see any of the men that had been at the Dom's Haven. *That doesn't mean they haven't sent someone else to grab you.* With my inner voice full of fear, I shuddered walking quickly over to the lift.

Was I imagining things because of what happened?

Possibly.

Isaac didn't seem worried about me being alone, so should I be?

Entering Mark's office a few minutes later, I let out a relieved breath at having made it on my own without incident.

"Hey Ferron. You're looking a little flushed today, you okay?" asked Helena, giving a friendly smile as always.

Over the last few appointments I'd started to chat with her while I waited, finding her to be as quirky as her hair, which was currently bright purple. "I'm fine. I was rushing, that's all," I lied, hoping she'd let the matter drop. I'd only taken two steps towards the familiar pink padded seats when Mark's office door opened and he appeared.

"Oh, perfect timing as always, Ferron. Come on in." Mark stood back to allow me to enter. Today's suit was beige with a kind of washed-out green shirt. I bit my lip to stop the urge to tell him that it did nothing for his complexion.

"Helena, can you give my wife a ring and tell her I'll be running about an hour late tonight? Thanks." He didn't wait for a reply before closing the door.

I took my normal seat, shutting my eyes as I carried out the mental exercise of putting the crap I carried around with me in the bin by the door. There was the sound of leather creaking, but I ignored it as I focused on emptying my mind.

By the time I was done, Mark was sat opposite me with his fingers steepled under his chin. His gaze was thoughtful. "That took you a little longer today, Ferron. Has something happened?" His brows rose, but other than that his position didn't change.

I chewed on my thumbnail trying to figure out what I wanted to talk about first. "A few things have happened since I was last here"—I scratched my ear—"and it's hard to figure out which of them I want to talk about."

"Which do you feel is the most important?"

"Isaac." it popped out before I could think about it, Mark's lips twitching.

"There you go. Let's start there and see where it leads us."

I sat forward, resting my elbows on my knees. "Isaac took me on a date." I sucked in a shaky breath before carrying on in a rush. "I tied him to the bed. He was naked and... I did stuff to him." The wave of heat that rode up my face could have warmed the whole room it was that intense.

Mark didn't bat an eyelid as he waited to see if I'd finished. His face stayed neutral, whereas I was sure that my mortification from talking about this was clear for him to see.

As the seconds continued to tick by, I gave a heartfelt sigh. I'd had too many previous appointments not to recognise what Mark was doing. He was giving me time to decide if I wanted to elaborate further before he asked a question.

"Were you naked too, Ferron?"

I barely kept myself from dropping my gaze as I shifted uncomfortably in the seat, my fingers pressed against my bristly jaw. "No, I wasn't. Isaac never even suggested it. Do you think he might have been put off when I told Phil what had happened to me?" Mark's furrowed brow made me tug at my hair. "Sorry, I'm confusing things."

"It's fine, Ferron. Just take a second and do me a favour, visualise your happy place. Let's see if that will centre you."

The calmness in Mark's voice made me all the more aware that I was feeling anything but. I dragged in a shaky breath and then another, letting Isaac's face appear in my mind's eye. My body immediately started to relax. "I'm going to try and explain everything in order so please bear with me."

I licked my dry lips as Mark nodded. "I can't remember if we discussed the impromptu stag party that Lenny held for Adam?"

"No, you didn't mention it."

I sighed mournfully. "That's where all my problems started. Lenny decided after Nathan went out for the day with Carl, Isaac and a few of the other Doms that he'd have a stag party for the other groom, Adam. He rang and invited me. I had a little meltdown about getting across London on my own and forgot to leave Isaac a note to say where I'd gone."

I went on to explain in detail what had happened. Once I got to the punishment part, my cock started to stir at the memory of what it had entailed. I skimmed over some of the details, even though I'd already talked openly about the sort of relationship that Isaac and I had. Some aspects were private though. When I'd finished, Mark's mouth hung open a little.

"Isaac's idea of a punishment was to take you out for an expensive meal, treat you to a movie you wanted to see, then get naked and allow you to take full control of what happened?"

He sounded surprised, and when he put it like that I could see why. I'd been so wrapped up in the word punishment that I hadn't thought about the details of it.

Isaac loves me.

Yes, you knew that.

But had I really? Had I really accepted what he'd said?

My chest swelled with the love that I'd been keeping hidden. "He loves me," I whispered.

"Yes, clearly he does. How do you feel about that?"

The quietly asked question was easy to answer. "Surprised. Amazed. Stunned, and so fucking happy! I never thought it would happen, that I'd find someone to love me after... after what Devon did to me." I sucked in a breath as a hiccupped sob escaped. "I'm scared to tell him how I feel."

A tear slid down my cheek as Mark gave me a sympathetic smile.

"You'll know when you feel ready to talk to Isaac about it. Don't be so hard on yourself. It sounds like Isaac is a patient man. He'll wait."

The ball of anxiety I'd been carrying around in my guts ever since our date released as I recognised the truth behind Mark's words. "Yeah, he is."

"Can we go back to what you said about Phil?"

I nodded, happy to be distracted from my gushing feelings.

"Did you talk about everything that happened at the Doms Haven with Devon?"

Why had I thought this would be a good distraction from Isaac?

Chapter Nineteen

Isaac

"What do you think?" Nathan enquired as he turned to face me.

Fuck, what had he been talking about? Was it about the incidents that kept happening? I swept my gaze around the messy, half-finished room. There was no way he could have been discussing the issues Boyd had been having over the last few weeks given the din from the workmen. The need to raise your voice to be heard ruled that possibility out.

Then what *had* Nathan been saying?

"You weren't listening, were you?" He heaved a sigh, dishevelling his blond hair as he shook his head

"Sorry," I mumbled contritely. "I've got a lot on my mind."

"You assured me that you didn't need to go with Ferron to his appointment," Nathan stated in an irritated tone.

"He's fine. I told you that Phil has one of his men following him when he's not with me. I'm not worried." Nathan's brow arched and he got an incredulous look on his face. "Okay, maybe I'm a little worried, but that's not what I'm concerned about. It's…" I licked my lips, glancing around to see how close the men were.

"You're blushing. Oh, my God, you're honest to God blushing, right now." Nathan roared with laughter and slapped me on the back so hard that I jolted forward. "The bear has finally been tamed. God, I love it."

"Fuck off," I said, but it was only half-hearted because he wasn't completely wrong. I had been tamed by my sweet little man and I didn't care who the fuck knew it. But with no idea who'd been sabotaging the second-floor renovations, I didn't want someone I didn't know knowing my business. "Let's go back to your office and we can talk in private."

"You really weren't listening, were you?" He huffed as he stepped closer. "Sam Villard, the guy who's applied for the bar manager position in the Flamingo Bar, has asked to come and have a look at the place. It's why we came up from the bar, remember?"

I rolled my eyes at the dramatic tone he'd used to jog my memory, heat filling my cheeks. "Yeah, okay. As I said, I've got a lot going on."

"Hey, there's a dude standing by the door trying to

get your attention," said Brett, Boyd's foreman, as he walked past lugging a tool box.

I glanced over to the door, but Nathan was already beckoning him over. My head tilted to one side as I took in the odd gait with which the man walked towards us. His blondish-brown hair flopped over his forehead as he scrutinised the floor, carefully navigating around the various objects scattered across it. He was around six-foot, lean, but with a broad chest, the jacket he wore straining at the seams as he tried to keep his balance.

I held my breath as what I suspected was a prosthetic leg caught on a bit of debris. He quickly righted himself, a dark stain covering his tanned cheeks. There was a defiant look in his dark blue eyes as he met my gaze square on.

Nathan held out his hand. "I'm Nathan, this is Isaac, the bar manager from The Playroom."

"I'm Sam Villard, thanks for meeting me." He took Nathan's large hand and shook it before offering his hand to me. "Nice to meet you both."

His gaze moved between Nathan and me, assessing us before taking in the room. Nathan fidgeted at my side drawing my attention. My stomach dropped at the deep creases around his mouth and eyes.

"Have we met before?" Nathan asked, his gaze never leaving Sam as he swung his gaze back to Nathan.

"Once. You came to say goodbye to Serg and I was just leaving his office." There was something strange in his tone as he mentioned Nathan's old Sergeant, but before I could examine it further, Nathan was already patting the guy on the shoulder. He wobbled slightly and I lurched forward to steady him.

His eyes met mine, the light of defiance back in them. "I'm fine," he ground out, sounding ungrateful for my help as he pushed at my hands.

Only when I was sure he wouldn't topple over did I release his arm and step back. "I'm sure you are, but from one comrade to another we don't leave a man to struggle."

Nathan's brow rose and I shrugged at his nonplussed expression. He clearly hadn't worked out the reason for Sam's lack of balance. It wasn't up to me to explain though, so I folded my arms and said nothing.

"What am I missing here?" Nathan glanced between us before his gaze settled on Sam.

"I've got a prosthetic leg that I'm still getting used to. But it won't prevent me from doing the job," he said in a defensive tone, his face darkening as his gaze remained steadfastly on Nathan.

"I'm sure it wouldn't," Nathan stated, "but I'd like to point out that you haven't been interviewed yet."

I swallowed a chuckle at the contrite expression that appeared on Sam's face. He looked like an adorable puppy. What was his story?

"Yeah, sorry. I'm just trying to figure things out."

Nathan was more careful when he placed his hand on Sam's shoulder this time, his face showing compassion. A compassion that I understood now that I'd seen the scars Nathan's body held.

"If you wanna talk about it, I'm a good listener. We all

have our scars to bear." Nathan's voice thickened, but his face displayed no shame as he stared at Sam.

"Thanks." Sam choked out, blinking rapidly as he turned towards the bar. "You gonna show me around?"

Nathan's smile appeared pinched as he answered. "Come on then."

Two hours later after saying goodbye to Sam, I followed Nathan into his office. I got the sense that the interview would be unnecessary given all the questions Nathan had asked Sam while we'd toured the building.

After the one little mishap, he'd been sure-footed and had even shown off his titanium leg. I took the seat in front of Nathan's desk, waiting for him to confirm my suspicion.

"He's perfect, right?"

I grinned at Nathan. "You know, if I was a betting man I'd have put money on that being the first thing you said when we came in here."

"Oh, come on, he's got enough experience to work the bar. His time in the army must have given him some good people skills. He's a real charmer when he relaxes and, as far as I can tell, he's a submissive. Or he's at least into the lifestyle in some way. There's something about him..." Nathan shook his head. "Not that that's relevant obviously, but it's definitely a plus. What do you think?"

"I think you're right. He'll fit in well." I held my hand up as Nathan went to interrupt. "But if you decide to offer him the job, you'll need to think about the space at the back of the bar. Regardless of his ability to do the job, and I don't doubt he can, he's going to need some adaptations to help him get through an eight-hour shift, or longer. Those adaptations are going to be tricky to implement because I think he's stubborn and will see it as failure. So be warned."

Nathan's expression was thoughtful as he tapped a finger on his lips while staring at me. "Yeah." He sighed. "It's going to be a bugger. I'll speak to Boyd and see if there's any way we can figure out a way to make it work for Sam without it being too obvious."

I laughed at Nathan. "When are you going to ring him and put him out of his misery?"

Chapter Twenty

Ferron

I tutted and shook my head as I yet again migrated from the lounge to the kitchen to stare at the chart. The neatly written rows of rules caused my heart to leap with joy.

Rule 1: To ask for what I want (Ferron)

Rule 2: Be honest with Daddy when I'm upset (Ferron)

Rule 3: No touching without permission (both)

Rule 4: Talk honestly about what's on your mind, no matter what it is (both)

Rule 5: To have a phone with you at all times (Ferron)

Rule 6: List punishments for when Ferron is naughty (Isaac)

Rule 7: Spend an hour every day cuddling (both)

Rule 8: Daddy is in charge of bath time (Isaac)

Rule 9: Remember it's okay to say no (Ferron)

Rule 10: Take charge of all Daddys' orgasms (Ferron)

Rule 11: Share a bed (both)

The last one that we'd added this morning was by far my favourite, okay second favourite after rule ten.

The sound of the phone ringing pulled me from my thoughts. Thoughts that in the past three weeks, had been filled with adding rules to the chart. It hadn't been as easy to create as I'd initially thought, taking several attempts as I'd plucked up the courage to express myself just as I'd discussed with Mark.

He'd helped provide clarity about the whole situation, including what might happen with the police. I'd never considered the fact that the things I'd told Phil might lead to having to talk to the police if he uncovered more information. I tried not to think about it though, too worried about how it might change things. The current case against Devon centred on the kidnapping and assault. The police weren't aware of the rest of it. I'd had a few sleepless nights thinking about how they might react to my confession after all these months. Would they think I was a liar?

My finger traced the rules as a distraction. Rule eleven, as of tonight, would have me in the same bed with Isaac for the entire night.

A grin spread across my face until my cheeks ached. Oh God! All the tiny hairs on my body stood to attention as a full body shiver coursed through me. It was as if they were already anticipating what was coming.

"Are you looking at that chart again?" Isaac asked from behind me, his voice full of humour.

I jolted, my hand falling to my side as I turned around with my cheeks hot. "Maybe." I shrugged, trying to act nonchalant.

The tip of Isaac's middle finger ran down my nose as he smirked. "You love the latest addition to the rules, don't you?"

I fluttered my eyelashes. "Which one? The one where I'm in charge of making you come? Do you mean that one, Daddy?" If it was possible, my smile widened even more at his resigned expression. "Actually, the one I'm excited about"—I stepped closer until there wasn't any gap between us and he could feel my excitement—"is where you have to let me sleep in your bed," I whispered on a breathy moan as I pressed against his warm, scented body. "I think that will be my favourite." It was the truth. The other one was just icing on the cake.

He groaned, pushing me away slightly so that he could adjust his cock within the confines of his trousers.

"Now Daddy, I think that goes against rule number three. No touching unless I say so." I gave him a smug smile as he shook his head at me.

"You're a bratty boy, do you know that?"

"Yes, but you love me anyway." As the unguarded comment slipped free, my hand flew to cover my mouth.

My hand was promptly removed from my mouth, Isaac's lips replacing it. His mouth was hot and possessive as I opened up, his tongue sliding against mine. His taste flooded my senses, arousal stirring to life in my groin. The moment of panic I'd had was obliterated as Isaac deepened the kiss until all there was, was him, the feel, the smell, the taste.

By the time he'd stopped kissing me, my whole body thrummed with need. Need I was getting used to experiencing whenever he touched me.

"I do love you, every little thing about you. Don't ever doubt it. I even love your bratty side, but if you tell anyone I said that I'll deny it," he said in a jokey tone. He winked, releasing me to walk over to the counter and switch on the kettle.

I bit my tongue to stop from sighing. We'd agreed when we came up with the list that the first rule was that I had to ask for what I wanted, and regrettably that also included sex.

When I'd discussed my fears with Mark, he'd been in favour of the chart suggested by Isaac. Mark's thoughts on the matter were clear—that I could use the rules to help me figure out when I was ready for the next step. That way Mark had explained, there'd be no second guessing for either Isaac or me. In principle that was great, unless you took into account the fact that I sucked at asking for what I wanted.

The one time I'd tried to do that with Carl, it had been an absolute disaster. When Isaac had asked me to go to Carl's wedding as his date, I'd had to navigate around that. As much as I'd wanted to go on another date with Isaac, the idea of it being Carl's wedding hadn't sat well with me. Not when I still had issues with everything that had happened after he'd rejected me. I didn't blame him, and I loved Adam, but I had baggage which wouldn't be helped by going to their wedding. So I'd worked and sulked instead.

Mark had been helping me to work through the mental block of Carl's rejection sending me down the path in the first place. I stared at Isaac's broad back. "Why can't things be simple?"

"Simple how, little man?"

I groaned, only realising as Isaac responded that I'd spoken aloud. I gazed at him, his concern evident in his grim expression.

"I didn't mean to say that out loud."

"What provoked it in the first place?"

The sound of the kettle bubbling filled the silence as it lengthened and I tried to come up with an answer other than the one that had been on my mind.

Isaac's head tilted to one side, his eyes narrowing on me. He pointed at the chart on the wall. "Rule number four, you need to talk honestly about what's on your mind."

The firmness in his voice wasn't cruel but it was authoritarian, my shoulders sagging. "I... I was thinking about the... past." The heat that spread up my face and all the way to my hairline, scalded my skin. There was no way to hide it when Isaac stood mere feet away from me.

His brows knitted together. "Do you want to talk about... it?"

At his obvious hesitation, tension crept up my shoulders and into my neck. "I... well... you see... yes!" I cringed, working hard to keep my gaze fixed on Isaac's.

The frown lines on his face deepened as he gave a slow nod. "If that's what *you* want?"

I didn't miss the way he stressed the 'you' part before carrying on making a cup of coffee. When he asked if I wanted one, I declined, knowing that my stomach would refuse anything right then. I went and sat at the table, seeking a way of being able to talk about what I wanted without sounding like a complete idiot. That was why I'd embraced submission in the first place because it had left me free to just be while my Dom took charge.

After Devon though, that was no longer an option for me. At the end of my last session with Mark, we'd discussed how the idea of even trying to do a scene with Isaac made my skin crawl regardless of how loving he might be. Mark had made me realise that the Daddy/Boy dynamic between Isaac and myself was a new way of expressing the submissive side of me.

That was all well and good though, until it came to asking Isaac to touch me, and I didn't mean in the bath or the shower when he washed me. Although those moments made my heart soar as he expressed his care through gentle touches, there wasn't the heated desire I was starting to want more and more.

When Lenny had come to the club the night before, I'd confided in him that I was worried that now that Isaac knew everything he maybe didn't want to touch me sexually. He hadn't poked fun at my concern, instead pointing out how often Isaac made excuses to touch me.

It happened so often that I'd not even noticed it until Lenny brought it up. I'd spent the rest of the night counting how many times Isaac had touched me. A lot, was the answer. In fact, too many to count as it had turned out.

Was I ready to let Isaac do more?

Chapter Twenty-One

Isaac

My nerves stretched to breaking point at the sight of Ferron's hand absently tracing over the grain of the wood of the kitchen table, his gaze unfocused. The last three weeks had been some of the best but also the worst of my life. The best because every step that Ferron took towards asking for what he wanted gave me hope that one day he'd see himself as I did: a beautiful courageous boy. But with every brave step he took and as he gained a little more confidence each day, it ripped at my self-control like nothing else could. With each time that he chose to touch me, to hold on to me willingly, to show how his body reacted to mine, it made it harder to continue to go at his pace. A pace that even a snail would probably mock.

Yet, I couldn't find fault with it when moments like this happened, when he became bratty and unguarded. It revealed parts of Ferron which had been hidden by the devastation of his past. In those moments of witnessing the confident boy he was turning into, I lost a little bit more of my heart to him.

My lips twitched at the memory of how bratty he'd become over the rules. He'd turned the tables on me in spectacular style. I'd been upset when I'd woken after our date to find that he wasn't lying beside me. It had been hard to act normal the next morning when all I'd wanted to do was demand to know why he'd not returned to me. So I'd rung Mark to seek advice, something I was sure the man was going to start charging me for soon. As always, he'd advised me to follow Ferron's lead and, boy oh boy, had that been worth it when he'd sat down with me this morning to ask if he could add something to our chart.

Initially after taking it off the wall, Ferron had sat staring at it as if it might bite him. He'd chewed the end of the pen for several minutes while pretending not to look at me from beneath his eyelashes. Then as he'd started to write my heart had lodged in my throat.

Rule 11: Share a bed (both).

I was sure that the grin that had spread across my face had made me look dopey, but I hadn't given a fuck. I'd wanted him to know how fucking happy I was with his rule. I wanted to give him a world of love where he got everything his heart desired.

Although that didn't help me to get him to talk freely about Devon.

Since the meeting with Phil, I'd kept my thoughts and feelings to myself. I was sure that Ferron didn't want, or need, to carry my baggage as well as his own. As the weeks had dragged on without him saying anything, I'd stupidly thought he might never want to talk about it with me.

I heaved a sigh at the way the universe had decided to bitch slap me today. Ferron had just happened to talk openly without prompting on the very same day where I needed to talk to him about Nix and the security team I'd hired. Something I'd steadfastly avoided initiating a conversation about, but I was now going to have to confess.

Mug in hand, I walked over to the table and took the seat next to Ferron, his gaze remaining firmly fixed on the table. It was a sure sign that he was uncomfortable with what he wanted to say.

Mouth dry, I took a big gulp of the steaming coffee, feeling it sear my mouth. The heavenly flavour lingered on my tongue as I marshalled my thoughts, but then they all fled as Ferron's gaze lifted to meet mine. His eyes were deep pools of longing that stole my breath away. Needing to distract myself, I took another sip of the scalding hot drink.

"Do you want to have sex with me?" he whispered hesitantly.

The sip of coffee I'd just had splattered on the table as I spluttered and choked on the burning liquid. I placed the mug down on the coffee-stained table with shaky hands. *What? Holy shit! Did he just mention... sex?*

My thoughts ran into each other as I wiped my mouth and stared at Ferron wide-eyed. He fidgeted in his seat, chewing on his thumbnail.

"Little man, where did that come from?"

He rolled his eyes heavenward. "My mouth," he quipped back so fast that I couldn't help but chuckle.

"Are you giving Daddy cheek?" I raised my brow aiming for stern and failing miserably, amusement in my voice.

His cheeks turned an adorable shade of pink as he pouted. "A little... but... but you never answered my question, Daddy." His chest rose and fell so quickly that it looked as if he'd been running.

"No, I didn't and I'm sorry, but you kinda threw me for a loop there."

"Daddyyyyy, you're still not answering me," he whined.

My lips twitched with the effort of not laughing at him when he was so adorable. But he was right. I hadn't answered him because I wasn't sure he was ready for my response. *Trust him, like he trusts you.*

Exhaling a shuddery breath, I reached for his hand on the table, lifting it away from the spilt coffee. "Come and sit in Daddy's lap." Ferron didn't hesitate continuing to hold my hand as he waited for me to push the chair back and make room for him.

His weight settled on me like a warm blanket of joy as he draped himself over me. His hand moved as it always did to the centre of my chest, rubbing at my T-shirt directly over my heart. He nestled his head in the crook of my neck as he snuggled into me. He fit so perfectly against me that if I'd have been a whimsical person I'd have said that he'd been made specially to fit me. Okay, I did feel like that at moments like this as his clean scent filled my senses, his firm body touching mine.

His breathing settled as I stroked his hair, his body relaxing fully against me. "How long have you known me, Ferron?"

He tensed briefly but didn't lift his head, clearly unsure where I was going with it.

"Over three years."

"That's right, and in that time did you watch me play with subs at the club?" This time he did lift his head, his brow marred with deep lines.

"Sometimes... I... I don't like hardcore BDSM," he whimpered, shifting as if he intended to get up.

I could feel his heartbeat vibrating through his body. I carried on stroking his back gently until he calmed. "There's a side of me that enjoys those elements of play, little man—"

"I... can't do it... I can't," he cried, not giving me a chance to explain fully. He buried his face in my chest, his body shaking in my arms and tearing a hole in my heart.

You stupid fucker, just spit it out so that he understands!

"Look at Daddy, please. Little man, look at me," I begged, my voice thick with emotion.

The sight of his tear-stained cheeks gouged at my heart. "I know that, Ferron. I've always known. I'm only talking about it because that's the only picture you have of me when it comes to sex, and it's not the one I want with you. We need to talk about it so that when we do have sex, you're not worried about it."

He swiped at his eyes with the back of his hands and gave me a hopeful smile. "You mean that, Daddy? That I... I don't have to do..." he trailed off, gulping, his Adam's apple bobbing several times as his face developed a pink glow.

"Absolutely," I rushed to reassure him, an idea already forming. "How about we use the chart to help decide what you'd like Daddy to do to you?"

His cheeks still held bright splashes of colour as his eyes sparkled with a dancing light. His bottom wriggled against my groin. "Can I add to the chart with things I'd like to do to you?" His voice trembled, but it wasn't from fear judging by the excited expression he now wore.

I groaned. "You're going to make me suffer, aren't you?"

He clapped his hands together, bouncing a little harder against me which increased the pressure on my groin. Any thought of talking about what I'd come to find him for earlier was buried under need, under the desire to give Ferron exactly what his eyes begged for: me.

Chapter Twenty-Two

Ferron

At the prospect of a day with Isaac which didn't include work, I'd talked myself into having a conversation with him about something I wanted adding to the chart. But what we were about to add to the chart wasn't what I'd expected. The day was fast becoming one of the best days I'd ever had.

Excitement buzzed through me as I skipped upstairs to retrieve the coloured Sharpies from my bedroom, Isaac moving around in the kitchen. *It's not your bedroom anymore.*

With my heart in my mouth, I struggled to swallow, rubbing my slick palms against my jeans.

We were going to add sex things to the list. Holy fuck!

At the top of the stairs, I grabbed onto the railing, hoping the wave of dizziness would subside.

Don't overthink it. Seriously, you're getting what you want.

Yeah, but could I go through with it? Could I get naked and let Isaac touch me, touch my arse?

I blew out a breath, all the unanswered questions making me feel even more lightheaded.

At the sound of the doorbell, my head whipped up so fast that I had to clutch at the stair rail before I could muster the strength to peer over it. Why did someone have to show up now? At the sound of Isaac cursing loudly, my brow wrinkled, the urge to stomp my foot disappearing.

Was he upset because of the lost opportunity too? His reaction seemed a little over the top though considering how patient he usually was.

Isaac's feet thudded heavily as he moved from the kitchen and came into view. My stomach quivered as he hesitated at the door, his hands repeatedly running through his hair.

Then his head turned and his gaze met mine. There was such an array of emotions running across his face that it was hard to catch what they all were. But the one I did recognise—regret, made the nervous excitement I'd been feeling disappear.

Before I could say a word, he'd turned back to the door and opened it to reveal Phil and a blond, tattooed giant. My eyes widened at the sight of the blond, the hairs on my arms standing to attention. Had I seen him before?

Bile burned the back of my throat as Isaac didn't ask what they wanted, instead stepping aside to let them in.

I gripped the railing and didn't bother with the pens as I walked back down the stairs with a sense of dread in the pit of my stomach.

"Can you guys go into the lounge and wait? I need a minute with Ferron," Isaac asked. Both men walked down the hall and disappeared out of sight. The sound of a door closing had my feet moving.

"Daddy, what... what's going on?" I hated how anxious I sounded, but the eerie feeling I'd kept having when I was alone outside had returned when I'd laid eyes on the blond man.

"Phil you know, and the guy with him is Nix. He's one of my oldest friends and works with Phil's security team."

Isaac took hold of my hand and led me away from the closed door and into the kitchen. My sense of foreboding increased as Isaac released my hand and stepped away. His hands balled at his sides as he met my gaze with some trepidation. "Please don't be mad at me," he begged, making my heart go back into my mouth and try to choke me. "I hired Phil and his men to watch the house to keep you safe. One of Phil's men has been watching over you ever since the stag party." His cheeks darkened as he stared at me.

He's had men watching me! All this time, he's been protecting me.

As the thought sank in, my initial shock gave way to a wave of love so bold and strong that my whole body shook. Misunderstanding my reaction, Isaac swept me off my feet and into his arms, burying his face in my neck. His scent enveloped me as his arms tightened around me, the muscles flexing. My feet dangled in mid-air, his hot breath making my skin tingle. "I'm so sorry, I should have told you. I just wanted to keep you safe. I came to talk to you about it earlier, but then we got distracted with, well, you know over what. I love you so much that I couldn't bear it if something happened to you."

Isaac went on and on, trying to justify something that had melted my heart. *This whole time he's been protecting me. This whole time.*

A giddy sensation coursed through me as I wrapped my arms around Isaac's neck. "I love you." The words bubbled out desperate to be heard. My mouth dried up, my heart taking flight in my chest.

Isaac's entire body seemed to freeze for a moment. He lifted his head, his dark eyes seeming to take up his whole face as they widened. "Say that again," he said, his voice a husky whisper filled with raw emotion.

"I love you, Isaac. I love you." I peppered his face with kisses as I continued to repeat the words, the joy lighting up his face so bright that it almost blinded me. It was like looking directly at the sun.

"Oh, little man." The reverence in his voice caused a ball of emotion to lodge in my chest. Tears stung my eyes as he lay his forehead against mine.

"I wasn't sure I'd ever know what it was like to be

loved, to love someone with everything that's inside me. But you've taught me differently, Isaac. I'm sorry that I haven't said it—"

"Don't apologise for taking the time to figure out what you wanted. We all have to do things at our own pace. I'm over the moon that you've shared your feelings with me. Fuck, if I could I'd shout it across the Downs that my boy loves me."

All I wanted to do was cherish the moment. Was it selfish of me not to want to spoil it by talking to the men in the lounge? I swallowed a sigh. "Why are the men here, Daddy?"

His eyes closed and he sucked in a breath before opening them again. "They want to discuss what they've found out about the Dom's Haven and how that affects you, Lenny and the court case."

The distress in his voice somehow helped me to keep it together, knowing that he needed me to be strong. He needed me to be brave for him as well as myself. I kissed his mouth softly. "It's okay, Daddy, I've got you and we'll do this together."

"You bet your arse we will. We'll fight and win." His response quelled a few of my nerves, but not all of them. As if he'd sensed that I wasn't ready to let go of him yet, he encouraged me to wrap my legs around his waist.

He carried me into the lounge without a word. I couldn't see either man so I wasn't sure what their reaction to Isaac carrying me was, only that it was silent in the room. Right then, I didn't care because I felt safe and protected.

Isaac settled in his favourite spot on the couch with me nestled against his chest. His rhythmic breathing helped to keep me calm and stop me from running from the room and hiding.

"Sit the pair of you. You'll make Ferron nervous standing over us like that." Once they had, Isaac's head tilted towards the man he'd called Nix. "What did you find out?" I was grateful for Isaac getting straight to the point until the guy started to speak and my heart trembled in my chest.

Dear God, there were others! There were others like me!

Tears burned my eyes and fell down my icy cheeks.

Chapter Twenty-Three

Isaac

Any excitement at being able to hold Ferron in my arms all through the night had been overshadowed by his intermittent and mournful sobbing. It had left him hollowed-eyed as he got ready to come to work with me. I'd considered getting him to stay home, but the mere idea of leaving him on his own now that I knew what those bastards were capable of had kept me from voicing the suggestion.

It didn't matter how many times I cursed myself for not speaking to Nix and Phil alone, it didn't make a blind bit of difference. For two excruciating hours, we'd sat and listened to Nix and Phil go through all the gory details. Details that had confirmed my suspicions about there being other men suffering out there. Men who were just as vulnerable as Ferron had been, who were alone in the world and had been treated as the Doms' personal possessions instead of human beings.

Ferron had been inconsolable as they'd laid it all out, crying for those men. He was the only one of us who truly knew what the men had had to endure and I'd have done anything to protect him from it. But he'd refused to leave once Nix had started to talk.

Every tear that had dripped off his chin and onto my hand may as well have been blood because they made my heart bleed. I'd felt useless at being unable to stop him from hurting.

"Isaac, if you continue to hit the punch bag like that, there will be nothing left of it," Nathan stated warily.

I swiped at the sweat dripping from my forehead as I gazed at him. "Put your gloves on then and climb in the ring with me." I pointed to the ring beside the now lopsided punch bag, which was still swaying from the brutal thumping I'd just given it.

Before Ferron had moved in with me, I'd used Nathan's personal gym frequently. He'd been generous with providing access to it, but I'd only ever used it when he was there. Over the years, Nathan and I had sparred together. I'd done a little boxing in the past, but I wasn't as fast as Nathan was so I tended to avoid getting in the ring with him. But with the anger inside me not abating, I wanted to hit something that would give me a little more satisfaction.

"You must be in a foul mood if you're actually offering to be my sparring partner?" Nathan's blond brows rose as he remained at the side of the punch bag. He'd been busy when I'd arrived at work that morning and then Ferron had been around so I'd not had a moment to talk about the day before.

With Ferron occupied showing Sam the bar set-up downstairs, I'd taken the opportunity to steal a few minutes to decompress. Only the more I'd punched the bag, the angrier I'd got. It seemed to have robbed me of my sanity as I pushed at Nathan. "Come on, just a couple of rounds."

He eyed the raggedy sweats I wore from the bag of workout clothes I kept there. "No. You're soaked with sweat which means you've been hammering at the bag for a while. I won't take advantage of you in your moment of weakness." His brow quirked. "But I'll keep the offer in reserve for when I need a punch bag."

"Fuck off," I ground out, but without any heat. Now that the adrenaline was wearing off, it was easier to admit that he was right. My shoulders ached like a bastard and my arms felt as if I had sandbags attached to my wrists.

"Go and shower and I'll grab us a drink. Then you can tell me what's up." The resignation in Nathan's voice said that he suspected that whatever I was going to say would fuck with him and Lenny too. He wasn't wrong. Ferron's horrific experience had caused a ripple effect that was going to leave none of us untouched.

Showered, but only feeling marginally better, I walked down the hallway and into the lounge. Nathan was sat at the breakfast bar nursing a half-full glass, a full one on the counter next to him.

Once I'd joined him and sat down, Nathan gave a resigned sigh. "This is about the Dom's Haven, right?"

I nodded, picking the drink up and swallowing it in two greedy gulps. My hand shook as I placed the glass down and met Nathan's worried gaze. "They have a slick operation going on. They get the subs to fill out a form online. It doesn't ask for a lot of information, which to me is suspicious, but to a novice or someone who's upset about something, you could easily miss that all is not quite what it seems. Then they invite the sub in. That's when they wheedle out the vulnerable. If they haven't declared any family members, they get taken straight to the manager's office. This is where it gets interesting. From what Nix has found out, it seems that the Doms interested in paying for a sub of this kind also fill out an application. Then when a sub turns up that meets their needs, they bring them to the office and hand the guy over. Job done." My teeth ached from grinding them together in order to keep control of the seething anger churning in my stomach. The nauseous feeling had been easier to cope with when I'd had Ferron to focus on. Now it made me want to heave as I swallowed the bile.

"Motherfuckers!" Nathan got up and stalked over to the window, his whole body seeming to vibrate as he stood with his back to me, his hands clenching and unclenching the entire time.

"That with fucking bells on. Oh, and there's something else."

Nathan swung around, his jaw clenching as he eyed me with anger simmering in his gaze. "Go on."

"Do you remember Wren, Ferron's friend?" I wasn't surprised when Nathan nodded; he had an eidetic memory. "As you know, Gabriel's been going to the club for several months now and he thinks he's seen Wren. Gabriel believes he's one of the men being held against his will. He's not been able to get close to Wren, but I asked Nix not to mention it in front of Ferron. When Ferron spoke to Phil about how he'd found out about the club, Ferron mentioned it was Wren who'd suggested the place to him.

"That made me suspicious. Made me wonder if he'd set Ferron up? They seemed pretty tight as friends though so I'm thinking not. If that's the case then I'm wondering if he went looking for Ferron when he disappeared." I rubbed the back of my neck. "It was only after I realised that I hadn't seen Wren for months that my gut told me it wasn't a coincidence. Is he still paying for his membership here?"

Nathan's brows merged as he tapped at his lip. "He pays a year in advance. I'm pretty sure that his payment is due next month. The end of it, I think. I'd need to double check my records to be sure." His expression remained thoughtful as he pursed his lips. "Do you think there are others that come here that might have got themselves caught up in this mess?"

The genuine concern in his voice made a restrictive

band form around my chest as he voiced my own thoughts aloud. "I think it's time we checked the records to see who hasn't been around for a while."

Nathan's face was grim as he gave me a curt nod. "You'd better get back down to the bar before Ferron starts to worry. I'll go through the files and talk to you later."

My sense of dissatisfaction wouldn't leave as I headed into the bar. The second I stepped into the room, I searched for Ferron. He was standing behind the bar, the lights above him making his hair shine. It flopped into his eyes as he shifted to look over at Sam. He swiped at it absently while answering whatever question the other man had asked.

My eyes burned with emotion as I stared at him. I was starting to get used to them rioting inside me though. The love I felt had blossomed into something so bold and beautiful that it matched my man perfectly. He was so brave and so gorgeous that he made my heart soar. To the point where I couldn't even contemplate how devastated I would be should something happened to him.

He believed that I was the strong one, but he was wrong. I hoped that one day he'd come to the same conclusion on his own. Until then though, I'd make sure that he understood that he was my forever and there was nothing I wouldn't do for him—nothing.

I sucked in a tremulous breath as I walked towards him, hoping that what I offered would be enough.

The End... until the revelation

Coming soon, the final instalment in Ferron and Isaac's story. Read on to get a little sneak peek from the next book.

SNEAK PEEK FERRON'S JOURNEY; PART THREE, REVELATION

Isaac

The weight of Ferron's stare was like a physical touch as he twisted in the seat to face me. "Does it bother you?" he asked hesitantly.

Taking my eyes briefly off the road, I glanced at him. "No, but then I'm older and have lived more of my life." Eyes back on the road, I held my breath while I waited to see what he'd say. He'd seemed confused and I wasn't sure why.

"What's that got to do with anything, Daddy? Age is what? A number decided by how many birthdays someone's had? How does that determine what you think or feel for someone? What I feel can't be measured by a number. I'm not sure it can be measured at all because it's so huge."

He sounded so genuinely mystified that I chanced another glance at him, my heart stuttering at the love shining in his eyes. I gave him a big grin, taking a hand off the steering wheel to squeeze his thigh. "I love you."

"If that's the case, then stop asking me silly questions. I love you too. It's as simple as that. I don't need to justify it, so why do you?"

That told me!

From out of the corner of my eye, I saw him shrug, his cheeks turning pink. I squeezed his thigh again, pretending there weren't ten thousand gushy feelings swarming inside me. "I'm sorry, you're right. I'll stop being silly."

I caught his eye roll, his lips twitching. "I'm not sure that's possible," he muttered under his breath but still loud enough for me to hear.

"Are you being cheeky, little man?" I asked in a serious tone while working to keep the laughter at bay.

"I'm not sure I can answer that without incriminating myself so I'll plead the fifth."

The laughter I'd been struggling to contain filled the car at his bratty response. God, I loved it when he acted out. He knew that though and the little bugger loved it. It was the best medicine and always lightened my mood.

The remainder of the car journey was filled with a companionable silence which released some of the kinks in my shoulders. By the time we'd pulled into the club's underground car park, I was already going through the list of jobs I needed to do.

Distracted as I parked in my designated spot, a flash of movement nevertheless caught my eye in the side mirror. What was that? My gaze swept the large garage as

I parked up, reaching for my seatbelt before I'd even switched off the engine. I released it quickly, keeping my movements slow and measured as I used the rearview mirror to check behind us.

Was there someone lurking in the garage?

I couldn't see anything, but the tiny hairs on the back of my neck stood to attention as other senses started to kick in. "Ferron, I need you to stay in the car for me, okay?" I kept my voice even, not wanting to cause him any alarm.

When he twisted his neck to look at me, I could see that he'd picked up on my unease though. Other than the movement of his head, he was rigid in the seat, his eyes as round as saucers. Recalling what I'd said to him, I cursed under my breath. I'd called him by his name. Fuck!

"What is it?" he asked, barely speaking above a whisper.

A lie sat on the tip of my tongue and I had to bite it back. *The truth, he needs the truth.* "I think I caught movement behind the car as I parked up. I'm going to go and check it out. I want you to pull out your phone and if anything happens, *don't* get out of the car, just call the police." I put as much emphasis on him staying in the car as I could as I glanced around the shadowy car park.

The contractors' cars and vans scattered around the space offered a multitude of hiding places.

Ferron nibbled at his lower lip. "Could it be Nix, or one of the other men you've hired?"

"No, they only follow if I've got to leave you on your

own." Ferron's face fell and his chin trembled. "It's going to be fine as long as you do what I said." Only once he'd nodded did I open the door and get out.

I locked the car as soon as I was out of it, focusing on my surroundings rather than a wide-eyed Ferron. Taking a few seconds to block out the external street noise, I listened for anything out of the ordinary as I scanned the surrounding vehicles. A scent of car fumes and dirt didn't give any clues as to whether there was anyone else there. Yet I sensed there was someone there, someone watching and waiting.

A scraping sound came from my right-hand side and I pivoted in time to see an ugly fucker with a scruffy beard coming towards me at speed, a crowbar in his hands.

With no time to think, I spun around, kicking out at the arm which held the weapon. His face registered surprise at my speed as he yowled, the metal bar clattering to the tarmac. There was no time to grab for it as the guy bellowed in anger and launched himself at me.

The air left my lungs as we collided with the car. It rocked and I used it to propel myself forward, bringing my knee up hard enough to make him taste his dick at the back of his throat. He grunted as his legs gave way. A surge of adrenaline pumping through me, I pulled my arm back and landed a solid punch to his jaw. His head snapped back before lolling forward, his eyes rolling back in his sockets.

"Fucking piece of scum!" I shook him hard enough to

make his teeth rattle, dropping him to the ground as I registered Ferron's cry.

My eyes narrowed on the other guy who was attempting to use some sort of carjacking device to open my car up. His focus was on the job he was doing rather than on his friend who was now laid out cold. My knuckles cracked at the wide-eyed terror on Ferron's face. This guy had no idea what a huge mistake he was making but he was about to find out.

Books by the Author

<u>Standalone</u>

When Fake Changed Everything

<u>Series by JP Sayle</u>

Billionaire's Playground:

Property of a Billionaire (Book 1)

The Flamingo Bar:

Always More (Book 1), also available on Audible

Potters Creek Series:

A Christmas Wish (Book 1)

The App Series:

The App: Daddy Kink (Book 1), also available on Audible

The App: Littles (Book 2)

La Trattoria Di Amore Series

Puzzle Pieces (Book 1)

Dominated but not Subdued (Book 2)

The Playroom Series

Mine, Body and Soul (Part 1), also available on Audible

Mine, Body and Soul (Part 2), also available on Audible

Mine, Body and Soul (Part 3), also available on Audible

Ferron's Journey, Part One: Damaged (Book four), also available on Audible

Ferron's Journey, Part Two: Hidden (Book five), also available on Audible

Ferron's Journey, Part Three: Revelation (Book six)

The Manx Cat Guardian Series

Where it all Began: Origins (Book 1)

Seeing Beyond the Scars (Book 2)

Destiny Collides (Book 3)

Searching for a Soul to Love (Book 4)

The 12 Disasters of Christmas (Book 5)

Laws of Attraction (Book 6)

The Teacher's Boy (Book 7)

About the Author

Hi all,

My name is Jayne and I live in the Isle of Man. A tiny place in the Irish sea. It's an island steeped in folklore and history and just begs to have stories written about it, and one of my true inspirations.

I've been happily married for over 25 years to a wonderfully complicated man, and I have a wonderful daughter with two very young grandbabies. I am also an identical twin, so if you see me, check, as it may not be me.

I have written contemporary and historical gay romance with a paranormal twist, daddy kink, fake boyfriends, out for you and enemies to lovers. My head is so full of ideas. I never know where it will take me next. I have a twelve book plan for this year and already I've a few new ones bubbling inside me waiting to be written ☺

I hope you have enjoyed this book, and if you are in need of more, then you can find all my other books, on Amazon and in KU.

If you're interested in keeping up to date with what I'm planning then why don't you follow and join me on the following links.

You can find me and follow me on:

Newsletter Sign up:
https://bit.ly/33bjgB3

Goodreads:
https://www.goodreads.com/user/show/39039955-jayne-p-sayle

Tumblr:
https://jaysayle.tumblr.com/

Bookbub:
https://www.bookbub.com/profile/j-p-sayle

Instagram:
https://www.instagram.com/jaynepaton/

Twitter:
https://twitter.com/JPSayle69

Facebook:
https://www.facebook.com/JaynePSayle

If you would like to give me any feedback or just have any questions, go ahead and friend me on Facebook, and I would be happy to answer anything. Well, almost anything. I hope you enjoyed this book as it was a little different for me. If you would also like to leave a review, then I would love to read your thoughts.

Thank you for taking the time to be part of my dream.